She couldn't let the man simply die on her couch.

The only thing she could do was pray. She swallowed hard and put her hand on the man's chest, right over where she was pretty sure his heart was, shut her eyes, and prayed aloud: "Please, dearest God, make him well and whole. Please. Please, God. Bring him back to health."

She could feel each of his ribs as his chest rose and fell with every labored breath. He was as thin as his shirt.

She opened her eyes and looked at the man again. Whoever he was, he seemed to be teetering on the edge of life. "Stay alive," she whispered to him.

There had to be a reason God had brought him to their home. Maybe in time she'd know, but one thing she'd learned in her nineteen years was that God had His own timetable, and it might not be until she was in the great hereafter that she would learn the whys and why nots of life on this earth.

In first grade, **JANET SPAETH** was asked to write a summary of a story about a family making maple syrup. She wrote all during class, through morning recess, lunch, and afternoon recess, and asked to stay after school. When the teacher pointed out that a summary was supposed to be shorter than the original story, Janet explained that she didn't feel the readers knew the characters well enough, so she was expanding on what was in the first-grade reader. Thus a writer was born. She lives in the Midwest and loves to travel, but to her, the happiest word in the English language is *home*.

Books by Janet Spaeth

HEARTSONG PRESENTS
HP458—Candy Cane Calaboose
HP522—Angel's Roost
HP679—Rose Kelly
HP848—Remembrance

Kind-Hearted Woman

Janet Spaeth

Heartsong Presents

To my good friend Colette Riely.
You are a truly kind-hearted woman.

A note from the Author:
I love to hear from my readers! You may correspond with me by writing:

Janet Spaeth
Author Relations
PO Box 721
Uhrichsville, OH 44683

ISBN 978-1-60260-593-0

KIND-HEARTED WOMAN

All scripture quotations are taken from the King James Version of the Bible.

All of the characters and events in this book are fictitious. Any resemblance to actual persons, living or dead, or to actual events is purely coincidental.

Our mission is to publish and distribute inspirational products offering exceptional value and biblical encouragement to the masses.

PRINTED IN THE U.S.A.

one

He has answered me! He can't live without me! He tells me
that we belong together, that we will breathe and live and
love as one. When I read his words, of how he will carry me
away from this drudgery, I want to spin in the barnyard.
Never mind the chickens. I am Cinderella, and this is no longer
Minnesota, 1935, and the drought is only—

Lolly Prescott smiled as she reread the words. He was wonderful, truly he was. He was everything she'd always wanted, everything she'd dreamed of. She shut her eyes and clutched the journal close to her. Her heart was in the paperbound volume, her secret love revealed.

Her reverie was broken by frantic barking from outside, signaling her brothers' arrival back from the fields. The family dog never let the two young men out of sight, and the beast barked the way some people talked—without end. If it weren't for the furry protective love Bruno provided, she would have long ago traded him in for something quieter.

She shoved the notebook into her apron pocket. The notebook had been a gift from her teacher when she graduated from high school. It was no bigger than a slice of bread, and was bound in plain brown card stock, but it had become her haven. Hurriedly she stuck the pencil into the bun straggling down her neck. She didn't dare let them know about her secret. They'd never give her a moment's peace—not that they did anyway, she thought, as the dog danced happily around her feet.

"George. Bud." She tried to calm her voice. "You're back early."

Her brothers threw their hats at the rack in the hallway, both of them missing the hooks and leaving the hats on the floor. Automatically she walked over, rescued the headwear from Bruno's playful tossing, and hung them properly.

"It's hotter than—" Bud began, but George prodded him with a warning shake of his head. Bud glared at his older brother. "What did you think I was going to say? Give me a little credit here, George."

"I know it's hot," Lolly said, trying to stave off the argument that would inevitably begin if her brothers weren't sidetracked. "This whole summer's been dreadful. Do either of you want a glass of water?"

"Is it boiling?" George asked, pulling a chair from the table and dropping into it.

"Not yet. Ask me again midafternoon. It just might be by then, especially if it sits in this kitchen." She poured water into a dish for Bruno, who promptly lapped the bowl dry.

"Awww, poor Lolly. Is my poor sister feeling put upon? Is it too hot in here? Want to try a turn in the fields? Think it's cooler there?"

"Stop your blathering, Bud. It's too hot for that kind of nonsense." George leaned back and put his arms over his head. "I wish the air wasn't so still today."

A fat fly buzzed sluggishly on the window ledge. She pushed a stray strand of hair, wet with sweat, back to the bun at the nape of her neck, but it promptly fell out again. "It might rain."

Bud hooted. "Might rain. Might snow. Hey, George, it might even hurricane!"

Lolly shut her eyes just long enough to send up a short prayer for patience. All these years of living with her two brothers, especially Bud, had given her plenty of practice in the art of the brief prayer.

Bud was nearly seventeen, but his impetuous energy made him seem younger. He sped through life without caution. When he was four, he jumped from the hayloft to see if he could fly. He couldn't, and the scar over his ear was silent testimony to that experiment.

At seven, he decided he wanted to know what it was like to drive the truck. They had to rebuild the chicken coop after that escapade.

Now, ten years later, he was still as rambunctious and un-contained as ever.

George, on the other hand, was a somber and proper fellow. He seemed to Lolly to be stolidly middle-aged rather than twenty-four. He was, Lolly had to admit, a bit boring.

"Anything coming up in that weed patch you call a garden?" Bud asked, interrupting her thoughts. "I'm about ready for some sweet corn and green beans and some big, ripe tomatoes. That's the stuff dreams are made of."

She rolled her eyes. "Dream on, then. So far I've got radishes. Want some radishes for dinner? How about for breakfast?"

"You two are crazy. Radishes just come up first. Give her some time, Bud."

George unfolded his lanky frame from the spindle chair and made his way to the door. "I'm soaked, and I smell like a barn. Just because I stink doesn't mean that the kitchen should, too. I'm going to clean up before dinner."

He preferred to use the pump outside to clean himself off rather than the sink inside after working in the fields, especially in summer when the water was cool from the well and evaporated almost immediately in the heat.

From her position in the kitchen, Lolly watched him at the

pump. Lately the water hadn't been coming out of it as easily as before. No matter how hard she tried, there were times when she couldn't get any water out at all.

But George was stronger than she was, and water soon gushed out. That was a good sign. It meant that the water table was still high enough for them to use. Nevertheless, George, always careful, made sure that every drop went into the catch basin.

Her brothers were so different from each other. George lived by rules and expected everyone else to. Bud was a bundle of lightly packaged energy. There was nothing about the two that was alike, except their nearly obsessive sheltering of their sister.

As if she had anything to be sheltered against here in Valley Junction. Lolly resisted the urge to sigh. There wasn't a marriageable man within fifteen miles of her, unless she counted seven-year-old Adam Whitaker, or Nigel Prothus, who was well into his nineties.

One thing this drought had done was to take away what few choices she'd had. When she thought about it, a heavy blanket of sorrow lay across her. So she did the only smart thing. She didn't think about it at all, at least not unless she had to.

Usually there wasn't enough time to dwell on anything. Taking care of the farmhouse and the scattering of chickens took up most of her time.

She touched the little notebook hidden in her apron pocket. Everyone needed some kind of dream. Dreams were choices.

If anything, she needed the light that her dreams provided. She felt stuck, right in the middle, both in age and in managing her brothers. Stuck on the farm. Stuck with her brothers forever. Stuck with a dog that would not stop barking.

When her parents had died in an accident five years ago, the responsibility for the family had fallen directly on her young shoulders. She'd been barely fourteen at the time, and she'd grown up very quickly. Too quickly.

The fly on the windowsill stirred slightly, and she noticed others beside it, on the outside of the house. In the distance, somewhere near the river, a mourning dove called, and she lifted her head with hope. "Did you hear that?" she asked Bud.

He shook his head. "It's all folklore, and you know it."

"No, it isn't." One thing she'd inherited from her father's side of the family was the same streak of stubbornness that made Bud such a trial at times; except she'd learned—usually—to keep her composure. Bud, on the other hand, was pigheaded and strong willed, and it was only through the grace of God that he hadn't ended up in some kind of major trouble.

She could still hear her mother's advice as clearly as if she were speaking it beside her: *We choose our battles, Lolly-Dolly. Be wise.* So she crimped her mouth shut and turned away, back to the window.

It wasn't folklore. It was real. Flies congregated on walls and mourning doves cooed before rain.

Her heart lifted with a momentary anticipation. Maybe it would rain. She closed her eyes, linked her fingers together, and began to pray. *Rain. Please, dear God, let it rain. We need—*

Her conversation with God was interrupted as something pulled on the back of her head, and her hair tumbled down around her shoulders in a sticky mass.

"A pencil? Why do you have a pencil stuck in your hair?" Bud waved it just out of her reach. "Let me guess. You're writing a book! That's what my sister's doing. She's writing a book! Hey, George! Guess what Lolly's doing!"

Hot anger mingled with cold fear. She watched as Bud let the screen door slam on his way out, and listened as he told

George, who shook his head soberly.

Her fingers closed around the notebook. There was no way she would share it with her brothers. She'd sooner eat every page than let them see its secrets.

She needed the comfort of her words. If she could build this story in her mind, it became, for a moment, a window. No, not a window. It became a door, a full-fledged exit from a relentless reality into something glorious and shining and beautiful.

Bud was talking animatedly to George, waving his hand in the air as if he were writing fanciful letters. His words floated to her through the torn screen door. "Look at me. I'm a famous writer. Here's my story. Once upon a time there was an ugly girl named Lolly."

"Cut it out," George said flatly. "Leave her alone."

Bruno barked at Bud, and her younger brother, diverted for the moment, threw a stick for the dog to retrieve.

Lolly let herself breathe easier.

He was just teasing. Of course he was. How could he possibly know? There was no way.

❧

Colin Hammett stopped and leaned against a sun-bleached fence post. The sun was relentless in its assault. He pulled a grimy handkerchief from his pocket and wiped the sweat from his face.

There'll be times you'll try to remember this heat, Hammett, he reminded himself. *Mentally bottle this and put a strong cork in it, so when December rolls around with its bitter winds and its stinging snows, you'll have this summer's excess to warm your hands and your soul.*

He almost laughed aloud. All this time on the road alone was making him quite the poet. Next thing he knew, he'd be penning sonnets about stars and odes to squirrels.

He'd changed so much in the past two months. He rubbed his chin and grimaced at the growth of beard. How long had it been since he'd shaved? One week? Two?

He was a mess. There was no doubt about it. He'd thought that his time on the road would give him some time to think, to sort things out, but now he knew even less than he did before.

When he'd left New York, he hadn't had any idea at all what he was getting into. He knew he had to get away, and get away he did.

His life there had been good, too good. The challenges were few, mainly which tie to wear to which soiree.

His company, a family business, was still successful despite the hard financial times that others had experienced.

He dropped his pack and flexed his fingers. He was very tired, but he needed to remember why he was here. Consciously, he began to run the scene again in his mind.

He'd been in one of the poorer sections of the city, in a hurry, as always, to leave it. He'd volunteered to drop off a carton of food, donated by his church, at a soup kitchen.

That had been his life—not unaware of poverty but untouched by it. And always, always, he'd prayed for the poor. Perfunctory prayer perhaps, but there was a part of him that held back compassion. Was it possible that there were *no* jobs, no employment out in the world? It made no sense to him.

He'd been especially rushed that afternoon. An evening dinner with the mayor beckoned. A ragged man seated at the door of a shop caught his attention, and in his expression, Colin had seen not the vacant gaze of despair, but eyes full of—of something. He hadn't been able to put a name on it.

The action was easy. Reach in his pocket, pull out a handful of coins, toss off a quick "God bless you," and be on his way. He'd done it a million times.

But this was the millionth and one.

"God bless you," he'd said, and the man looked at him with what he now knew was dignity and responded, "Blessed is the man that trusteth in the Lord."

At first it hadn't made sense, and Colin had dismissed it as the ramblings of a vagrant. But the words had stayed with him, digging into his bones until he finally faced the truth: He hadn't trusted in anything, especially not in God. He saw how meaningless and empty his life was, and he vowed to quit letting his life be given to him on a silver platter. The only way to do it was to change it all. If he was going to understand the man on the street, he'd have to become the man on the street. It meant starting over, with nothing.

The prospect of change was exciting. He'd come back from his expedition a changed man, with a backpack of stories to tell.

He went home, threw a change of clothes in a bag, and headed off to find himself.

Now he wished he'd been a bit more circumspect in his actions.

As he'd done so many times before, he ran through the litany of what he'd do differently. He'd have brought more money, arranged for lodging, settled his meals, organized some transportation, even packed additional clothing. He lifted up his right foot and stared ruefully at the sole of his shoe. It flapped loose and had a hole in it the size of a silver dollar.

But haste has its own wings. He'd flown out of the city, vowing never to look back. Here he sat, somewhere in Minnesota, by the best of his reckonings, and without a penny to his name—and he was indeed looking back and reevaluating his actions.

The life of a rambler hadn't been as exciting and invigorating as he'd envisioned. He'd managed to cobble together enough food and shelter at each stop to make this adventure bearable. It hadn't been easy, but that was part of the challenge.

The road shimmered in front of him, and he reached for a fence post to steady himself. Each step was becoming harder to take. Maybe the end of the road was near for him.

He'd always claimed himself as a Christian. He was a bulwark of his church, in the front each Sunday. Tithing and singing and serving as the president of the men's league—it all counted, didn't it?

When he'd decided to adopt the life of a vagrant, it was to understand those less fortunate, to become aware of his own blessings, and to get closer to God. He had succeeded on the first two counts, but on the last one? Unless he counted that he was pretty much knocking on heaven's door at the moment, he'd have to say he'd failed.

He took the canteen out of his pack and raised it to take a drink. His hand shook, and the few precious drops of water remaining fell to the ground.

The moment had come to ask for help.

A few tears stung sharply at his eyes, and he dashed them away with the filthy handkerchief.

Help. He didn't want to ask anyone for anything, not any-more. That had been his motto, ever since his life—or lack of it—had sent him from the days that had been totally planned out, right into the dizzying unknown of a life on the road.

Only the weak asked for help. How many times had he heard that—or, God help him, how many times had he said that? Only the weak.

But he had to have something to drink, and soon. His lips were dried and cracked, and his tongue was so swollen that he could no longer sing his way along the road. Now the hymns were only in his mind, the lines and verses jumbled together. Just that afternoon he had tried to get through

"Rock of Ages," and he struggled in the middle of the second verse as the lyrics left him.

Left him! He'd prided himself on his knowledge of hymns, and now that, too, was leaving him.

Something was happening to his head. Not only was he becoming wildly fanciful and horribly forgetful, he was having difficulty keeping his eyes focused on the road ahead.

Now there's a metaphor for you. The road ahead. How can I keep my eyes on the path before me when I can't even see where I'm going?

The brilliance of the sun was blinding. He blinked, and blinked again. But still he saw through a white veil of blazing sunlight.

His head felt like an oversized empty ball on the top of his body. He was floating.

Had it ever been this hot? This airless? The truth was that today was blistering and dry, just like the day before, and the day before that. *Rain* was the prayer on everyone's lips.

A verse from Jeremiah sprang into his head, the same one the man on the New York City street had said to him, and he said it aloud: "Blessed is the man that trusteth in the Lord, and whose hope the Lord is." There was more after it, something about a tree by a river, but he couldn't recall it at the moment.

He had to trust. God saw him, trudging along the road. God would see to him. God would provide. He had to trust in that, but he knew one other thing: He had to help himself, too.

He took one last swipe across his face with the grubby cloth and took a deep breath. *Pull it together. You have work to do.*

Resolutely, he balanced his bedroll on his back and took a tentative step. His knees turned to rubber, numbly refusing to hold up his body. The world swirled into a dust-colored spinning vortex, and his legs gave out from under him.

As he sank to the ground, a carving on the fence post spun by him. It was a roughly scratched outline of a cat.

Kind-hearted woman. That's what it meant. Some hobo before him had taken the time to alert others that this farm housed a woman who would feed the homeless.

That was what he needed, a kind-hearted woman.

As the clouds took over his brain entirely, he smiled. More words from the Jeremiah passage came to him: *Heal me, O Lord, and I shall be healed; save me, and I shall be saved: for thou art my praise.*

❧

"Lolly!"

Bud and George kicked open the screen door and made their way to the front room, where they dropped a man onto the sagging cushions of the worn old couch.

"Get some water," George said as he examined the man's face, lifting his eyelids and feeling his pulse in his neck. "He's still alive, but just barely. Hurry, Lolly."

As she picked up the pitcher from the kitchen table, the man groaned. She poured some water into a bowl and carried it to the living room, putting it on the table beside the couch.

"Here," she said, handing George a towel she'd snatched up from the kitchen. It was one she'd embroidered—a teakettle with a smiling face. It seemed so incongruous here with a stranger unconscious on her couch.

Beside them, on the shelf next to the crystal vase that had been their parents', a Bakelite clock ticked away the seconds.

George splashed the water on the man's face and dribbled a few drops into his mouth. "He's dehydrated," he announced. "Look at his lips, how dry they are. There's hardly any liquid in him at all."

"Yeah," Bud agreed. "His canteen was on the ground beside him, sis, empty and dry as one of Bruno's bones."

"He hasn't had enough food or water to keep body and soul together," Lolly said softly. "He's so thin."

"Look at this." George pinched a bit of the skin on the back of the man's hand. "See how it stays up in this peak? That means he's really parched."

Lolly checked on her own hand. The skin spread right back to its original state. "I didn't know that was how you tested for dehydration. How'd you know that, George?"

He shrugged. "It was in the chickens manual I got from the county. Figure a body's a body, whether it's a chicken or a man."

"Did it tell you how to treat it?" Bud asked as he studied the man on the couch.

"I know we shouldn't give him a lot of food and water all at once," George said. "Just give him a small amount at a time, even if he wakes up and asks for more."

" 'Even if he wakes up'?" Lolly repeated. "He is going to wake up, isn't he? I mean, he's not going to, you know, well. . ."

"He'll be fine," Bud said, standing up and wiping his hands on his dungarees.

George moistened the tea towel embroidered with the smiling teakettle and wiped it across the man's face. "Why, he's just a young man," he said as the dirt came off. "No older than me."

Lolly's heart twisted as she looked from the man to her brothers. How lucky they were to be together, rather than living the life this poor man had been.

He groaned again, and the three stared at him.

"I believe we have company, Lolly," Bud said at last. "Bring out the fine china."

two

Together. It is the most beautiful word in the English language. Together. We are not meant to live apart, not when God has joined our hearts in timeless love. We will grow together like the well-watered vine, climbing up the trellis of the years. It is our destiny, our forever.

The three siblings stood around the worn sofa, watching intently as the man stirred. His face was ashen against the faded burgundy and green tapestry of the couch, his shoulders gaunt in the sunken cushions.

Breathe. Lolly stared at the man's chest, willing it to rise and fall. Breathe in. Breathe out. Breathe in. Breathe out. She realized she was inhaling and exhaling with him, as if her own strong lungs could give him air.

One of the neighbor's cows lowed from a far field. Bruno barked in response, and the chickens clucked among themselves.

The cows belonged to Ruth Gregory's family. George was, everyone assumed, going to marry Ruth one day, but he was slow to speak his piece. For the past three years, whenever he was in town, he'd dawdle at her café in town, sipping a cola. The cow was more vocal than he was, Lolly thought.

It seemed odd, almost as if there were two worlds existing side by side, the normal everyday one out in the field and the yard, and the drama unfolding in the house.

The stranger's mouth twitched, and his eyelids flew open, his gaze latching almost immediately onto Lolly. "Sah

17

kaahraah aah," he said, his eyes, as dark brown as George's coffee, not moving away from hers.

"A cigarette!" Bud said under his voice. "The man wants a cigarette!"

"No, I think he said he wants a cigar." George frowned at the stranger.

"How do you get cigar out of 'Sah kaahraah aah'?" Bud argued. "He's clearly asking for a cigarette, aren't you, pal? Do you want a cigarette?"

"Or a cigar?" George persisted, leaning in toward the man.

"You want a cigarette, don't you?" Bud shook the stranger's elbow lightly. "A cigarette, right? See, he nodded."

"Oh, will you two stop?" Lolly said, pushing her brothers away. "You're taking up all of his air, and besides that, we don't have a cigar or a cigarette, so what does it matter?"

"I suppose," Bud grumbled, "although I'm sure that's what he said."

"Sah kaahraah aah," the stranger said again, and this time his mouth slid into a faint smile that held for a moment and then slipped away as his eyes shut again.

"Well, no cigar for you, mister," George said, "at least not until you get your strength back."

I'm going to need Your help here, Lolly prayed silently. *I've got a fellow here who is in terrible shape, and then, well, I've got my brothers.*

A flurry of barks from the door and a clatter of claws on the wooden floor announced the arrival of the dog. Bruno pushed his way in front of them and sniffed the stranger, starting at the top of his head, going all the way to his toes, and then back up again.

Before she could react, the dog licked the man's face enthusiastically. The stranger didn't even flinch as the huge dog's tongue left a trail of slobber through the dirt that still encrusted the man's face despite George's ministrations.

"Get back, Bruno! Honestly!" She tugged at him and pulled him away.

The dog flopped onto the floor, sprawling out as if his exertions had tired him out entirely.

Lolly shut her eyes. *See what I mean, God? Even the dog is a daily challenge for me.*

"I wonder where this fellow came from," Bud said. "He looks like he's been on the road for quite a while."

"I'm going to go back to the spot where we found him and poke around, see if there's something that might give us a clue as to who he is." George whistled and Bruno sprang to alertness. "Come on, boy. We've got some investigating to do."

"I'll come, too." Bud stopped and looked back and forth between his sister and the man on the couch. "You going to be all right?"

"I think so." Lolly looked at their guest. "He doesn't look like he's got the energy to swat a fly."

"Well, if he lives—" Bud began, but George walloped him in the shoulder, stopping the sentence if not the thought.

"He looks to be a tough sort," George said gruffly, looking away as he said the words.

Lolly turned her attention to the man on the couch. He looked anything but tough. His skin's underlying pallor lent a blue-white tinge to his sunburned face, and his breathing was shallow and rapid.

She touched the back of his wrist, carefully, tentatively, and his fingers twitched in response. She pulled her hand away and tucked it behind her back, as if hiding it would undo the action.

The man muttered something and jerked his head back and forth spasmodically. Then he began to speak. Through his parched and split lips, unintelligible words, no more than broken syllables, spun out in a papery stream.

Lolly knew he wasn't talking to her. He couldn't even know that she was there, he was in such bad shape. His eyes clenched, as if squeezing away a bad image, but never opened.

Perhaps he was delirious. Her knowledge of medicine was minimal at best. The only things she'd had to deal with were the occasional colds, sore throats, and stomach distresses, and the treatment for those had been simply to let the illnesses run their courses.

Was that the wisest thing to do here? Should she call for the doctor? And how on earth would she pay for his visit?

She couldn't let the man simply die on her couch.

The only thing she could do was pray. She swallowed hard and put her hand on the man's chest—right over where she was pretty sure his heart was—shut her eyes, and prayed aloud: "Please, dearest God, make him well and whole. Please. Please, God. Bring him back to health."

She could feel each of his ribs as his chest rose and fell with every labored breath. He was as thin as his shirt.

She opened her eyes and looked at the man again. Whoever he was, he seemed to be teetering on the edge of life. "Stay alive," she whispered to him.

There had to be a reason God had brought him to their home. Maybe in time she'd know, but one thing she'd learned in her nineteen years was that God had His own timetable, and it might not be until she was in the great hereafter that she would learn the whys and why nots of life on this earth.

It wasn't that she didn't have questions. Why, for example, did good people suffer? Why did God let that happen? Why did their parents die so young?

Why was there drought? Why didn't He command the rain to fall? Why was the depression tearing so many lives apart? And when people were hungry, why didn't He send down some of that manna?

She sat next to the couch, matching the rise and fall of his chest, breath for breath, willing him to keep inhaling and exhaling, until frenetic barking and loud voices announced that her brothers and the dog had come back.

"We found it!" Bud called from the doorway, then clapped his hand over his mouth as he glanced at the prone figure on the couch. "Is he dead?" he asked in a stage whisper.

George pushed him aside. "You have the manners of a coyote," he informed his brother, "and you smell just as bad." Then, gently, to his sister, "How's he doing?"

"The same. What did you find?"

"Wait until you see!" Bud slid across the floor to her. No matter how many times she'd told him to stop, he insisted on doing it. He'd never grow up. The boy was almost seventeen and still acting like an adolescent. Lolly despaired of his ever behaving like a grown-up.

Automatically she chided, "Slide across that floor one more time, and I'll polish out the scratches with your head."

He waved away her complaints and held out a pack. It was dusty and soiled, and Lolly drew back. It smelled like, well, like a man on the road would smell.

"And George has got the fella's bedroll."

Before Lolly could interrupt the inevitable, Bud dumped the contents of the pack on the floor next to the sofa, and George untied the bedroll and let it unfurl. The end struck the little table with the bowl of water they'd used to clean off the man's face, and she caught it before it spilled.

"You shouldn't be doing that," she said. "That's just wrong, going through his things like that."

"It's not like he's in any position to give us permission," George pointed out. "And this might give us some important information, like maybe he's got some disease or something that we should know about."

"Some disease? There's a cheerful thought." Lolly shook her head. "Even if he had a disease, we couldn't do anything about it."

"Oh, do you suppose?" Bud asked, stopping his investigation of the contents of the man's pack.

"Do I suppose what?" Lolly asked.

"What if he has one of those terrible diseases that's really catchable—"

"Contagious," George said.

"Contagious, and now we'll all get it and die? And they'll come to find out why we haven't been to town for a month, and they'll find our shriveled-up bodies, and they'll realize that there are four bodies and only three of us, and it'll be a huge mystery who the extra—"

God, isn't it enough that I have these two buffoons to watch over, and now you give me an unconscious man, too?

George rolled his eyes at his brother and gathered up the blanket and flattened pillow that had been in the stranger's sleeping bundle. "Nothing here. I'll put it out on the fence to air out. Lolly, maybe once the bedding isn't quite so pungent you can take a look at it and see if it's worth laundering."

"Take this extra shirt and pants with you," Bud said, tossing the offending items toward his brother. "They're a bit heavy on the stink, too."

George paused before leaving the room. "So was there anything of interest at all in the pack?"

Bud shook his head. "There isn't anything in there, really. One of those free Bibles they give away and a comb and a toothbrush. I know, I know. Take it out of the house, too. Who knows what all is crawling on it."

Lolly looked at the man on the couch. His breathing had deepened, but it was still erratic. "He looks to be about your size, George. Do you suppose you could clean him up a bit more and get him into some of your old clothes?"

"Sure. Let me get his stuff taken care of, and then Bud and I will work on him. Come on, Bud, help me out."

The brothers left the house, carrying the stranger's things with them, and she turned to their silent guest, humming as she studied his face. She ran through hymn after hymn, singing the words when she could remember them, and letting the melody carry the song when she couldn't recall the lines.

He looked so frail, so helpless, lying there. His dark hair made the ashen color of his skin even more pronounced. He must have been on the road a long time to be this thin. His wrist bones angled out. Had he been hungry? Had to go without meals? Been forced to beg for food?

She and her brothers constantly battled the curse of need. There was never enough money, or maybe only just enough to keep them one step ahead of losing the farm entirely. They were still safe from this gnawing want that was plaguing the nation. At the very least, they had food. It wasn't fancy, and there were times when it wasn't very good, but at least it was there.

Was that why he'd come here? She'd fed other travelers in need, but they'd always thanked her and gone on. None had stayed. Of course, this man didn't have the option of choosing to stay or leave.

The verse from Hebrews sprang to her mind: *Be not forgetful to entertain strangers: for thereby some have entertained angels unawares.*

"Is that what you are?" she asked softly. "Are you an angel?" She shook her head. "I somehow don't think so, but angel or not, you are welcome to stay here and recover. We will take care of you as long as you need, whatever your reason for rambling is."

The Bible was on the floor, right where Bud had left it.

Typical of her brother, she thought, to leave it where it landed when he'd scrounged through the contents of the backpack.

More from idle habit than anything else, she opened the Bible—and saw a name written there in pencil. Colin Hammett.

"Is that your name? Colin?"

The figure on the couch didn't stir, and she picked up the pack to replace the Bible. It wasn't at all what she'd expected. The bag was made of fine leather and lined with beautiful lustrous fabric, although the piece hadn't weathered its time outside too well.

Someone must have taken pity on this man of the road and given him this bag to use. He certainly didn't seem the type to be able to afford it on his own.

One day he would tell her the story of his life. In order to do that, though, he'd have to wake up.

She sighed and looked at him. "One day at a time, Colin. One day at a time."

⁂

He wanted to open his eyes, to slide from this darkness back into the world. A woman's voice reached into the void, speaking his name. *Colin.*

An incredible thirst reached into his mouth and down his throat. He wanted to speak, and he tried, but the motion made his lips sting with nearly unbearable pain, and he slipped back under the edges of the darkness.

Waves. Sound came in waves, muffled, as if he were under the water at Jones Beach on Long Island. He was swimming, gliding through the dark waters. Overhead he could hear the cadence of conversation but nothing came together to form recognizable words.

Except his name. *Colin.*

Where was he? Who was speaking?

His brain wouldn't work, wouldn't stay on a thought. It skipped and skittered its way through his memories, searching for tags of something, anything, that could claim these sounds.

A dog barked. But that didn't make sense. It shouldn't be a dog. It should be a cat. A kind-hearted cat.

No, that wasn't right. Not a kind-hearted cat. A cat. A cat and a kind-hearted woman.

The barking was suddenly very close, and something slimy slurped across his face. Voices spoke sharply, and he was suddenly being lifted into the air.

His eyes sprang open, and the faces and shoulders of two young men were only inches from him.

"He's awake!" the older one said.

"Well, don't drop him," the other fellow said. "Lolly would kill us if we killed him, especially after we've saved him."

Every part of his head tried to piece together what his eyes and ears were telling him. None of this made sense.

"Lolly?" Colin croaked out.

"Hey, he's talking! Wait until Lolly hears about this! God does answer her prayers, I guess."

"Maybe she could pray us out of this drought, do you think?"

Colin had totally lost track of which one was speaking, as the exchange between the two men arced over his head.

"She hasn't left his side since he got here, except for now, of course."

Then a few of the stray bits clicked into place. A woman with long, light brown hair. Dark blue-gray eyes, the color of river-wet rocks. And a soft smile, a gentle touch, a quiet and true voice that sang—sang something he couldn't quite remember. But she had been there. "Ki-ha-wo?"

"What did I tell you, George?" the younger one asked. "He wants a cigarette."

Colin shook his head, an unfortunate action since it caused all the loosely connected fragments in his cranium to fly apart in a painful flurry. He shut his eyes again, closing out the world until the storm of pain could subside.

He was slipping back under the water at Jones Beach. The gentle waves were cool on his face, wet and refreshingly liquid. He could breathe under this water.

But first he had to say something, something that was very important. He struggled back to the surface and fought through the pounding that caromed around his skull.

He took a deep breath and focused every fragment into a fairly cohesive whole, and then he spoke. "Kind. Hearted. Woman."

Then, having said it, he let the water reclaim him.

ॐ

"He was awake, I tell you, he was," Bud said to Lolly. "And he asked again for a cigarette."

George swatted at his brother. "He did not. He said something, but it didn't make any sense. He said, 'Kind-hearted woman.'"

"Kind-hearted woman?" Lolly looked at their guest, prone on the sagging old couch. His eyes were closed, but his mouth was open a bit and his breathing seemed to be not as labored. Perhaps her brothers' cleaning him up had helped. The dirt had been sponged away, his hair washed and combed, and he was garbed in an old work shirt and pants that once belonged to George. "Why would he say that?"

"He's loco," Bud said. "He smacked his head when he passed out and he's probably got amnesia."

"Oh yeah," George said. "I forgot to tell you. He's got a big swelling over his ear. His hair covers it, but we found it when we were washing him up."

"He kind of yelped when I touched it," Bud volunteered.

"So George looked at it really close. There isn't any cut or anything, just a lump the size of your hand there. And it's an amazing color of purple, too."

Lolly knelt beside the sofa and gently pushed aside the man's hair. "His name is Colin," she said as she examined the wound. "Colin Hammett. I don't know if it's better or worse if there's no cut. At least it won't get infected, but it sure looks like he hit something pretty hard when he fell. I wonder what it was."

"He was over by the fence. Probably fell against the post. How do you know his name?" George frowned.

"I'm assuming it's his name. It's what's written on the flyleaf of that Bible." She smoothed the hair over the wounded scalp, taking care not to touch the swollen area. "He looks like a Colin. Did he have any other injuries?"

Her brothers shook their heads.

"Not that we could see, anyway," George contributed.

She bit her lip as she studied Colin's face. She knew absolutely nothing about medicine, but it did seem to her that he should have woken up. And since she knew now about the blow to his head, the stakes had been raised.

That much she was sure of. Head injuries could be deadly.

"We'd better get the doctor here." As soon as she said the words she knew that this was the right course, but how on earth would they pay for a doctor's visit? The only physician in Valley Junction was Dr. Greenleigh, whom Lolly knew solely from church. She had no idea how much he'd charge, but she suspected his services didn't come cheap.

"We can't afford a doctor," Bud said.

"We can't afford to let him die, either." George straightened their guest's collar. "I sure do hope that God is watching over this one. I really do."

You are, aren't You? Lolly asked God silently. *You are watching over him?*

She began praying in earnest, sometimes with words, sometimes without. George and Bud both left, and she only vaguely noticed. Colin had to live. He had to.

◆

Shadows crossed the room. Sunset came late on summer nights, but it started to creep across the horizon when she heard the rumble of the truck pulling up in front, followed by the smoother motor of an automobile.

The door slammed, and footsteps hurried across the floor to the couch.

"Lolly, let me take a look." Dr. Greenleigh perched on the side of the sofa. "If you all don't mind, I'll need some privacy. I'll tell you as soon as I know anything."

The three siblings left the room and gathered in the kitchen. Bruno followed them and sprawled on the floor next to them, chewing on something.

Lolly reached down and took the doctor's handkerchief out of the dog's mouth. "Nasty, Bruno." She'd wash it before she returned it. That dog. . .

Sudden tears filled her eyes. "You stupid dog," she said, fighting back the sobs that were building inside her. "Can't even leave the doctor's hankie alone." She swabbed at her eyes. Silly, crying over something like a handkerchief.

"He'll be fine," George said, but Lolly noticed the way his fingers were white where he gripped the back of a chair. "He'll be fine."

Bud shook his head. "I hope so. I don't want to be gloomy about this, but he's in really bad shape."

She knew that, but hearing Bud say it so baldly rattled her with unexpected force. Their guest had to live. He had to.

Her eyes stung as she fought tears. She mopped them away with the back of her hand as she lost the fight and great watery drops slid down her cheeks.

George put his arm around Lolly's shoulders, and she leaned against him, grateful for his strength.

Dr. Greenleigh called them back into the living room. "What this fellow needs is water. Start small at first and then build up, for the next day or so. Clear soup if you have some. Then add in food, a bit at a time. He may be ravenous, but it won't do his stomach any good to eat a lot right away."

"Eat a lot right away?" Bud echoed. "He's not even awake. How can he eat?"

"Bud's got a point, in a way," Lolly said. "I think I'd be glad if he just woke up. Why won't he wake up?"

The doctor nodded. "Well, he's tired for one thing. Exhausted. I'd wager that he hasn't had a good, restful sleep in quite a while. But he's also got a head injury, and that's tiring in itself."

"I thought people weren't supposed to sleep if they got conked on the head," Bud said. "I'd always heard that you had to keep them awake."

"He doesn't have a concussion, so it doesn't matter. But that doesn't mean he's going to sail on through this. Head injuries are mighty dangerous things." He looked at each of them slowly, one at a time. "The greatest danger, I'm afraid, is that he may lose all or some of his memory."

"But it'll come back, his memory that is, won't it?" Lolly asked, her hands twisting in her apron.

The doctor shrugged. "We would hope. The brain is an incredible thing. It has the remarkable ability to heal or to re-create new paths that go around the damaged area. Having said that, I do caution you that I've seen my share of brain injuries, and some people never recover."

"You mean they die?" Bud asked.

The doctor faced him. "Or sometimes the body stays alive, but the brain doesn't—or at least not much more than is necessary to sustain life functions. I can't say which is worse. That's not my call."

No one spoke until at last the doctor said, "Lolly, George, Bud, I'd recommend you pay close attention to him, and that you pray. What medicine can't do, God can. It's in His hands."

"Thank you, doctor," George said, as the physician clicked his medical bag shut and headed for the door. "How much do we owe you?"

The doctor paused and shook his head. "No charge. I can't imagine a more fortunate place for a man to almost die than here. If anyone can save him, the three of you can. The healing that's needed here isn't something medicine can do. No, it's up to you three—and God. I'll check back tomorrow."

The door closed behind him, and for a moment they stood in silence, stunned by the gravity of the task ahead.

"Well," George said, "no pressure on us, huh?"

Bruno barked at the doctor's car as it drove away. "He's quite the watchdog, that one," Bud said almost absentmindedly. "Barks when the doctor leaves."

"We should take turns watching over Colin," Lolly said. "If he wakes up—when he wakes up, someone needs to be at his side."

It was odd, she thought as she sat next to the couch later in the day, how things could change in a matter of minutes. And with those changes, how her perception shifted, too.

She'd felt caught, robbed of any choices she might make. And now, here with an injured stranger in her life, she was even more snared, unable to leave. But she no longer felt bound to the farm. She had a mission.

three

He is beyond what I ever could have expected. If I could dream a love story, this would be it. With him at my side, I feel light and carefree. I waltz on rainbows; I skip on clouds. The world is glorious with color, and melody surrounds me. He holds my hand, and we face the future. . .as one.

Her head bobbled on her chest as she fought sleep. She was so tired. George had slept right through his shift with Colin, but she hadn't had the heart to wake him up. He worked so hard to keep the farm going, and doing that while keeping Bud in line—or as much in line as possible—was difficult, and she knew that.

But she had to stay awake. What if Colin woke up? She couldn't let herself succumb to sleep. She had to stay awake; she had to.

A touch on her arm startled her.

She must have drifted off. The sun was up, and the dog was snuffling around her feet.

"Sorry," George whispered. "I guess I overslept."

"How is he?" She looked over at Colin.

"Better. He stirred a bit as I came in here. I wouldn't be surprised to see our patient coming to later on today, maybe even this morning. Why don't you catch a few minutes by yourself? You know, swab off, drag a comb through your hair, that kind of thing. Maybe even pop on a clean dress."

She couldn't bear the thought of leaving Colin's side, not when he might be waking up at any moment. "I'm fine."

"No offense, sis," George said, "but you're not."

"No kidding," Bud added as he joined them. "You should take a run by a mirror sometime soon, and then tell me if that's the first thing you'd want to see if you were returning from the world of the nearly dead. You, dear Lolly, are a mess."

There was no point in taking offense at anything Bud blurted out. What his mind thought, his mouth said.

And, in this case at least, he was right, she realized when she caught a glimpse of herself in the mirror over the mantel. The bun at the nape of her neck had almost entirely worked its way free of the string she'd used to hold it back, and now lank locks straggled around her face. Her dress was wrinkled and soiled from the day before. She wasn't a sight for sore eyes as much as she was a sight to make eyes sore.

She filled the basin in the bathroom and dunked a washcloth in it and began to repair the damage as best she could. Soon her hair, still wet, was pulled back in a respectable braid that was tied with a piece of blue ribbon, and she smoothed down the blue and white dress she'd changed into.

"Better?" she asked as she reentered the room.

"Lolly, we have guests. More guests." Bud's voice let her know exactly what he thought of these visitors.

Two women stood up from leaning over the couch. From the stormy expression on George's face, she knew that he wasn't happy. Bruno was growling softly outside the screen door, obviously not pleased at being exiled.

Lolly's heart sank as she saw who was gathered around the couch. She wasn't ready for them. Even with a good night's sleep she wouldn't be a match for them.

Hildegard Hopper had been widowed so long that the townspeople disagreed whom she'd been married to.

Whoever the mysterious Mr. Hopper had been, he hadn't lasted long into the marriage, but he'd managed to leave her well enough off that she'd never wanted for anything, even with the depression nipping at everyone else's heels.

Today her substantial body was wrapped in a spotless ivory dress, and she wore matching shoes with tiny curved heels and open toes. An absurd hat made of a scrap of wool, some netting, and a miniature bird's nest was perched atop her waved auburn hair.

Amelia Kramer was a tiny little thing, just the opposite of Hildegard, and within her gray-curled head were filed the town's secrets. Like a miniature human sponge, she absorbed everything that was said or done around her. Amelia reminded Lolly of a moth that fluttered around the brighter light of Hildegard Hopper.

Amelia had also dressed up for the occasion of meeting the mysterious visitor. She had on her Sunday best, a navy blue two-piece suit. Lolly knew from the design that once it had been quite expensive, but the seams had been repaired so many times that the cut no longer retained its original sharpness.

"Eleanor!" Hildegard tippy-tapped over to Lolly in her impractical shoes and embraced Lolly in a deep hug. Lolly tried not to inhale too deeply; Hildegard did love her perfume.

She winced as the heady scent invaded her lungs. Everything about Hildegard was simply too much: too much perfume, too much money, too much artifice.

And she called her Eleanor. Nobody called Lolly *Eleanor*, not since the day she was born and George had called her Lolly. Lolly she'd become—forever.

Lolly broke from the hug and summoned a smile for the women. "How sweet of you to come. I wasn't expecting you, but—"

"Oh, you goose!" Hildegard gushed on. "Of course you weren't, but we just had to come and see for ourselves! You are so nice to take this man in when you have practically nothing to speak of to live on as it is, not with this terrible depression taking its dreadful toll on all of us!"

"So nice," Amelia echoed. "So nice."

Hildegard minced back to the couch. "He's such a handsome young man. If only his circumstances hadn't brought him here to this lowly place."

George cleared his throat, and Lolly could tell that politeness was arguing with his desire to tell Hildegard Hopper what he thought of her calling their home lowly.

Hildegard must have noticed, for she clapped one hand over her mouth. "Oh, my dears, I didn't mean that! I meant his poor, poor condition, the state of affairs that placed such a man on the road, forced him to become a vagabond and to live off the kindness of strangers who might well not be able to stretch their own meager means to include him."

"Very kind of you to see to his needs." Amelia nodded as she spoke.

"Oh, these woeful times!" Hildegard fanned her face with her fingertips. "There isn't a body in the whole of Minnesota who hasn't felt the dreadful strictures of this horrible mess the nation is in, with no jobs anywhere and no money! Why, just the other day I was commiserating with Reverend Wellman about the sad state of the collection plate. One can hardly hope to keep house and home together, let alone give, as we all should, for the Lord's good work. It's a piteous time, indeed."

Amelia tsked in agreement. "Indeed, Hildegard. Wise, wise words."

"This poor man is indeed fortunate to have found you. Do you know what his situation in life is?" Hildegard's eyebrows arched inquisitively at Lolly.

"His situation?" Lolly asked blankly. "I'm afraid I'm not following you."

"His past. You know, what he was, what he did, who his people were."

Lolly moved a bit closer to Colin, and she noticed that her brothers leaned in almost defensively, too. "I'm sure I don't know," she said, trying to keep the coolness in her voice to a socially acceptable level.

"We're just concerned," Hildegard said, heading for her with opened arms again, "for your safety. With just the three of you out here, all alone, so vulnerable, orphans, the lot of you—why, it pains my heart just to think of the consequences that might occur."

Lolly stepped aside to deflect most of the hug. "We'll be fine."

"He could be a criminal," Amelia said in a softly sinuous voice. It was, Lolly thought, what a snake would sound like if it could speak. The woman's eyes were bright with anticipation, as if she hoped she was right and Colin might slaughter them all in their sleep. What a wonderful story that would be.

It was definitely time for the two women to leave before she or her brothers said something they'd regret.

Lolly placed a gentle hand on each woman's elbow. "He is still quite weak, so I think I'll ask you to return later. We are limiting his visitors and trying to keep the room as quiet as possible. I think you understand." She continued to murmur until she had steered the women out of the room and to the door of Hildegard's DeSoto. Bruno kept a wary eye on the group from the shade of the cottonwoods, occasionally baring his teeth at the visitors.

Without giving either woman a chance to interrupt, Lolly's

flow of words continued until the two women were seated in the vehicle.

"Perhaps another day? I hope so. Thank you so much for stopping by to see us. I hope you have a pleasant day."

She stood outside and watched as they drove away, perhaps, she admitted to herself, as much to make sure they were truly going.

When the last puff of road dust had vanished behind the stand of cottonwoods, she returned to the living room.

"How on earth did they know?" she asked her brothers.

"Well," Bud started out, and she knew she was in for a long story, "we went to the doctor's office to find him. You remember, you sent us to get him, so don't even think about blaming us."

"Bud—" she began, but he picked up his story, apparently anxious to clear his name.

"He wasn't there, so we went to the usual places we might find him. The bank, the post office, the church. Nobody'd seen him. George had to stop at the café, of course, and make lovey-dovey eyes at Ruth—"

"I did not!" his brother interjected, his face growing red at the mention of the young woman he'd been somewhat courting.

But Bud continued. "So by the time we got to Leubner's Store, word had spread that we were looking for him, and everybody of course thought you were sick or you'd cut off your hand or had died or something."

"Bud!" George broke in. "You can't tell a story straight for anything." He turned to his sister. "Let me tell what happened. We went into Leubner's, and we were asking if anyone had seen the doctor, and the next thing we knew, here he comes, wondering if you were all right."

"So," Bud interrupted, "we really did have to tell about this fellow here, and it couldn't be helped that Amelia the Snoop was there with her big old ears on; and next thing we know, everybody in town had heard."

Lolly sat down next to the couch. The smell of Hildegard's perfume hung heavy in the air, and she knew it also clung to her clean dress, courtesy of the hugs the older woman had given her.

"I don't like those two," Bud declared. "They were squeezing and poking our fellow, even wanted to look under his shirt to see how thin his arms were. I just don't like them at all."

"Oh, hush!" Lolly scolded. "You shouldn't say things like that."

"But if I say I do like them, I'm lying, and that's a sin, and you know it."

"You don't have to say anything about it at all. I don't recall anyone asking you what your feelings were about them." A bit of hair had fallen over Colin's forehead, and she brushed it away. She was feeling quite protective about him, and the fact was that she didn't want to share him with anyone else. Maybe later she would, but right now she wanted to make him better.

Bud shoved his hands in his pants pockets. "I guess I've got work to do outside. The farm isn't going to take care of itself, you know. Wheat won't grow on its own. Well, I guess it will, but I don't suppose anyone's got the eggs out of the henhouse yet, did they? Didn't think so." He whistled for the dog.

As he and George turned to leave, Lolly heard him mutter, "Hildegard Hopper. Bet that old woman's got a whetstone somewhere in that house that she sharpens her tongue on every morning."

Lolly looked down to hide her grin. It wouldn't do to let her brother see it. No, it wouldn't do at all.

&

Finally the room was quiet. Colin opened one eye a crack, just to make sure that they were gone.

He'd been asleep when suddenly a woman with a sharp voice like a cackling hen had bent over him, pinching his cheeks and pulling up his sleeve to examine his arm. Someone had pulled her away from him, but her voice clawed at his eardrums.

Her shrill voice kept on, until the woman with the gentle voice, the familiar voice, led her away. Her words were indistinct, but he could tell from her tone what she was doing.

Now they were gone, and the men, too. It was safe.

He opened his eyes. "Hello."

The young woman who'd floated in and out of his delirium jerked into alertness. "You're awake!"

"Sorry," he said. "I didn't mean to startle you."

That was what he tried to say, but it came out distorted. His words sounded thick and muffled. Something was wrong with his tongue. It seemed to be twice its normal size, and his lips didn't move like they were supposed to. He tried again.

"Excuse me. I'm having trouble speaking." The last words came out more like *lubble beeding*.

She leaned forward and ran her hand over his cheek. "Sssh. Let me get you a sip of water. That'll help."

She was the most beautiful woman he'd ever seen. Of course at the moment he couldn't recall any women he'd ever seen, but he was sure that when he could remember them, she would still rank at the top.

The water she dropped into his mouth from a spoon was like liquid grace. A few precious drops spilled out, and she caught them with her fingertip.

"Sit up." The words came out with remarkable clarity, and encouraged by that, he tried more. Slowly but distinctly the words formed. "I want to sit up."

"Are you sure?"

He started to nod but thought better of it when his head pounded in immediate response.

"I'll try," she said, and she leaned over. The smell of the sharp-voiced woman's perfume returned but under it was the soft aroma of soap, and a faint scent of shampoo.

She moved the pillows around and put her hands under his arms to lift him. "If I hurt you, let me know. I'll do my best not to, though. On the count of three? One. Two. *Three!*"

It felt wonderful to sit up at last. His body felt disconnected, as if his legs and his arms were no longer joined to his torso. He moved them experimentally and was relieved when feeling sparked back into the limbs.

"More water, please."

"Just a bit at a time, but yes, here's more."

She held the spoon to his lips again.

"I dreamed of water," he told her.

"I'm not surprised. You're quite dehydrated."

"I was swimming at Jones Beach."

She smiled. "I don't know what that is."

"It's on Long Island, in New York."

"That's quite far away." She lifted the spoon again. "More?"

"Yes, please. And I could breathe under water."

"Ah. That is quite a rare talent."

He was like a bottle uncorked. He couldn't stop talking, and the more he said, the easier it was. The words kept coming.

"You sang to me, didn't you?"

"Maybe. My brothers might argue if I sing or if I caterwaul, though."

"You sing. Like an angel."

She laughed at that, and the sound was like a crystal waterfall. "I think I should tell you that you hit your head pretty hard. I don't sound anything like an angel, I'm sure."

He couldn't stop looking at her. "What is your name?"

"Lolly. Lolly Prescott."

He nodded but checked the motion before it could set off the drums in his head. "Who's Eleanor?"

She grinned. "You were listening, weren't you?"

"Maybe."

"I'm Eleanor, but nobody calls me that, and neither will you. Not if you know what's good for you." She put another spoonful of water in his mouth.

"What happened?"

It felt as if he were waking up from a long sleep, which in fact, was probably true, he realized. Bit by bit his mind was starting to put all the little pieces together. But the effort of talking had worn him out, and he was glad to let Lolly speak for a while.

"My brothers, Bud and George, found you in the road behind our field. You were unconscious, and all you had with you was a backpack and a bedroll. They brought you to our house, and this is where you've been since yesterday, watched over by my brothers, our mutt of a dog, myself, and, of course, God. Somehow we managed to keep you alive. I think most of the credit goes to Him." Her lips curved into a slight smile. "All the credit goes to Him."

She settled back in the chair. "By the way, you're in Minnesota, not too far from Mankato. We're right along the Minnesota River. I don't know if you've ever been here before, but this is a lovely place, and I wouldn't trade it for all the riches of the city. The Minnesota is a golden river, especially in the fall when the leaves are touched with autumn and they fall into the water as it courses its way to meet up with other rivers, other streams. They're carried along like russet and bronze and copper boats, taking away the story of summer joy and making room for the icy splendor of winter."

Her words were spontaneous poetry, and he found himself hanging on every syllable. She sat back, and the images flowed from her like the current.

"You weren't too far from the river, and you may have heard the sound of it as it rushes toward Mankato, and then pushes up to join the Mississippi. I think it was calling you, and you heard its voice as it offered to give you relief from your thirst. When you're stronger, we can go to the riverside, and you can put your hand in the river, touch the water that saved your life. We will make little boats out of milkweed pods and send them on to Mankato and Minneapolis and on down to New Orleans."

He put his head back and shut his eyes again and listened. Her words flowed over him like the river, like the music of the river.

four

*Even though he has been away from me, away from my
arms, away from my embrace, he has never left my heart.
I think of him with each sunrise, and I pray for him at each
sunset, and when the moon rises high into the sky, a pure
pearl suspended against a velvet drop of ebony, I throw a kiss
to the orb that watches over us both as surely as our Creator
does. The universe wants us together, needs us to be together,
as surely as we need each other.*

The days passed, from June to July to August, with a wild
energy. Lolly's garden grew straggly in the afternoon heat,
but still she watered it each evening with hope. Bud pointed
out to her that maybe she should start watering it during
the afternoon, and that way the potatoes and carrots would
already be boiled when she dug them up for dinner.

Colin got better quickly—the doctor attributed that to his
youth and prior good health, but Lolly knew the real reason.
God had meant for Colin to survive.

His memory was spotty. Sometimes he could recall an
event down to the tiniest detail, and at other times, entire
events seemed to be missing. And of course, in between were
the spots where traces of his former life lurked, tantalizingly
imperfect and incomplete.

The gaps in his recollection frustrated Lolly, but she held
her impatience in check. His healing couldn't be hurried.

He had gotten, finally, to the point where he remembered
parts of his life: his name, where he had lived, and so on. He

had been in the family business in New York City, but exactly what that was, he couldn't totally identify. He'd told her he had brief flashes of a large building and desks and the distant sound of machinery, perhaps a printing company.

Trying to bring back the scenes of his past brought him to excruciating headaches, so they'd come to an easy accord: He would, at his own pace, explore the reaches of his memory, and she would listen as he shared the growing volume of his own history.

He had moved to the old house, a small building adjacent to the farmhouse. When her parents had first gotten married, they lived in the tiny place until their growing family needed more room, and they built the larger farmhouse. When Lolly was growing up, the old house had played many roles: a playroom, a place to dry pelts, a handy spot to store potatoes, and a catch-all for unused furniture. With the brothers' help, Colin repaired it and made it livable. It wasn't fancy, but it was good.

The wheat was starting to turn golden, baked too quickly under the summer sun, and he watched the crop as anxiously as George and Bud did, learning at their side the capriciousness of farming.

As soon as Colin had been able to, he'd joined them in worship at the little church in town. The townspeople of Valley Junction had taken to him, and with their usual good grace accepted him into the church community without reservation. Of course, Hildegard Hopper and Amelia Kramer were intensely interested in talking to him, but George and Bud were expert at moving him out of the women's sphere of nosiness. Her brothers knew how to keep the focus on worship.

Lolly was so glad to have them all together in God's presence each Sunday morning, and as this Sunday came with the usual August heat that shimmered from the ground to the sky, the church's windows were thrown open with the hope that can only come on Sunday that some breeze might find its way in. Ladies fanned themselves furiously, and men used prayer cards and announcement sheets, whatever they could find that made the still air move even a little bit.

Reverend Wellman was a tall, slender man with a slight limp. Born and raised in the area, he knew everyone and had an astonishing ability to tailor his sermons to the needs of the community—without casting an accusatory light on any member of the congregation.

His sermon was about the uniqueness of creation. Every one of us is different, he said.

He used the example of identical twins and told the story of his own brothers. No one, he said, could tell them apart. The doctor had marked them with his pen—A for the firstborn, and B for the second.

"Keep these marks on them," he'd told their mother and father. "That way you can tell them apart."

His mother had shaken her head. "I know them already."

The doctor tried some tests to prove to her the necessity of doing it his way. First, he had them dressed in matching buntings, with the marks covered.

She knew which was which.

He took them behind a curtain and she listened to their cries.

She knew.

He had her eyes covered, and laid each one in her arms.

She knew.

Now she was an elderly woman with failing eyesight, limited hearing, and a faltering gait. Her senses seemed to be abandoning her, yet she knew which son was which by touch alone, and sometimes by his mere presence in her room. She knew; even through the veil of the years, she knew.

That, Reverend Wellman said, was the way God knows his own. God wants us to seek out the qualities of each other that are special and to care for them, to know them the way God knows us.

Lolly sneaked a glance at Colin. He listened in rapt attention to the story the minister told, and when he'd finished with the sermon, Colin nodded, as if something had spoken to him.

The four of them sat together as they always did during every service, with Colin at Lolly's left side and Bud on her right, while George was perched on the edge of the pew.

Ruth, the woman who had George's attention—and his heart, if he'd ever admit it—sat across the aisle from him, her silvery blond hair glowing in the sunlight that poured through the open windows. Lolly suspected that George's attention wasn't always on the service. One day, she knew, either George would cross the aisle to sit with Ruth, or the reverse would happen, and she'd cross to sit with him, and they'd be as good as engaged.

Outside, Bruno snoozed in the shadow of the steps, keeping a wary eye open a crack in case an inattentive squirrel wandered too close.

Lolly had always enjoyed going to church. The music, the sermon, and the Gospel reading—all of those elements combined with the fellowship of the congregation kept the experience uplifting every week, a respite from the cares of the day.

Having Colin at her side made church even better. She told herself it was his strong baritone that the little church needed in the hymns, or his fervent *amen* at the end of the prayer, or his willingness to stay afterward and help straighten the sanctuary.

But she also treasured the way he held his Bible out to her

so they could follow the Gospel reading together. Why it mattered so much, she couldn't say, but it did. When he was beside her, and they were sharing the Bible he'd had in his pack, she couldn't imagine a Sunday without him.

He was, as Reverend Wellman's sermon had illustrated, very special, not only to God but to her.

He was still a man of contradictions in so many ways, and he wasn't able to reconcile them all himself. The blankets in his bedroll, she'd discovered when she'd laundered them, were woven from what she presumed to be cashmere or something similar. She was guessing, of course, never having seen cashmere, but these blankets were softer than any she'd touched.

The pack he'd been carrying when her brothers found him was made of fine leather, and the lining, although faded from days on the road, was a thick silken fabric with a golden brocade pattern woven into it. It had to have cost a dear penny, too.

Yet inside was that same Bible he shared with her on Sundays, a free Bible that had been given to him on the road. One afternoon he'd told her how he'd come to have it.

Her mind wandered away from the closing hymn, as she remembered the story he'd shared with her.

He'd been on the road, hitchhiking when he could, but generally walking and riding on freight trains, and following a set of railroad tracks on the theory that they would, eventually, take him to a city of some substance.

Sure enough, at last he'd gotten to a town in the upper Midwest—he didn't know the name of it—where he'd met some fellows in the rail yard. As a group of ruffians surrounded him, he'd heard the soft swish of knives being opened.

Suddenly an arm came out of seemingly nowhere, and a

loud voice announced, "I've got him now."

The thugs stopped their advance, and he was spirited out by his rescuer. It turned out that the fellow ran a flophouse for transients, and he'd put Colin up for the night.

But first he'd asked Colin if he was continuing on his travels, and Colin had said yes, he was. Would he like a road map? the man asked. Colin had nodded, and the man put a Bible in his hands, and said it was the best road map anyone could use.

It wasn't his first Bible. He remembered another one with pages he'd hesitated to turn because they were so thin they easily tore easily. He was almost afraid to touch it for fear of damaging the Word.

So this inelegant Bible, with its cardboard cover and thick rough pages, had been exactly what he'd needed.

He read it, he said, but not all of it, and he tended to turn to familiar passages, the comfort verses, he'd called them. Psalm 23. The Beatitudes. The Lord's Prayer. Those lines he knew.

He'd stopped speaking of it then. She suspected other memories were too nebulous to be shared, so she hadn't pried. In time he would remember—or he wouldn't. She couldn't change that, and she accepted it.

The benediction was pronounced, and the four of them filed out of the church.

George lingered for some small talk with Ruth by the front steps before joining the others.

"I'm sorry to say this in such a holy spot," Bud declared, "but that's not a nice place to be in August. It was so hot in there that the bird on Ruth's hat roasted, and it smelled so good that I was tempted to eat it."

"Oh, stop it," George growled. "That bird was made of wool, and you know it."

"I was simply making a point," Bud said. "You've got to admit that—"

"Boys, boys," Lolly chided, interrupting the inevitable argument. "Let's just get home. And Bud, watch what you say. That wasn't nice at all."

"How can I watch what I say? Words are invisible," he said as he climbed into the back of the truck. "I was just being honest. And by the way, I'm not going to crunch in the front with you. It's just too hot. Come on, Colin, you, too. It's more comfortable back here."

"When are you and Ruth going to go on a date or something?" Lolly asked her brother as he drove toward the farm.

George growled.

"Well, let me give you some female advice here. It's hard to get any kind of relationship going if all that happens is he looks at you. There's got to be more than that. Speak up."

"You're the big romance expert?" he asked. "Since when?"

"No, I'm not saying that. It's just that Ruth is nice, and I'd sure like to see you two together. But it doesn't look like it's going anywhere."

His eyes flickered over to her and he sighed. "I'll tell you what. I can't. I will not ask Ruth—or anyone—to share my life until I can take care of her the way a husband should. What would I do? Move her in with us? Or maybe we can boot Colin out of the old home place and she and I could set up house in there?"

"You could build a new house, George," she said. "There's nothing stopping you."

He didn't answer.

"Really," she persisted, "you could. Bud would help you. We can get the lumber here or maybe in Mankato, and with some nice new furniture, you'd be all set up."

"It isn't a good time."

"You're just shy." She loved to tease him about his slow courtship of Ruth.

"Things are too uncertain," he said, his mouth tightening, which always meant he was literally holding back his words. "The drought, the depression."

"But we're okay. We've got—"

"We've got enough for us," he interrupted. He glanced in the mirror at Colin and Bud behind them, horsing around, and lowered his voice. "You know that having Colin here has been a blessing, for sure, but it's also stretched us to the limit. We don't have reserves for a wedding, a new house, for furniture, and probably for children. I'm not bringing someone as classy as Ruth is into our chaotic bit of paradise."

She touched his arm. She hadn't thought about that at all. "I shouldn't have said anything."

He lifted one shoulder and let it drop. "No problem. It's a mess for all of us."

The rest of the ride was silent except for Bud and Colin singing silly songs from the back of the truck.

❧

The next day, the heat continued. She fanned herself as she stood in the kitchen by the open window and watched Colin with the chickens. Not a single breeze lifted the light curtain, and she felt a trail of sweat roll down her back.

She'd become used to seeing him in the farmyard, his dark brown hair under a worn straw hat as he strewed seed for the chickens, making *chhhkk, chhhkk, chhhkk* sounds at them while they scratched and picked their way through the bounty at his feet.

The chickens liked him, or so it seemed. Lolly shook her head at the thought. A chicken was a chicken, and it didn't do well for her to become attached to any animal on the farm that might end up on the table. Besides, chickens were such odd creatures, with their featherless feet and jerky head movements.

It had to rain, and soon. Even the light teasing showers that only misted the air would be welcome.

She didn't like weather like this, when the world seemed poised on the edge, as if waiting for whatever was coming.

It wasn't quite tornado weather. The sky was still too blue, not the sick green that indicated trouble was on the way, and the blanket of stillness that preceded a twister was absent. The chickens clucked and squawked territorially, Bruno barked in the distance at something—or nothing, knowing Bruno—and overhead a bird trilled out a melody.

But there were clouds. They were high and thin but they were there, and maybe, just maybe, they held moisture.

The sound of an automobile approaching intruded on the day. "Oh no, please don't let it be. . ." she said aloud as she wiped her hands on the dish towel. She hung it up again, making sure the smiling teapot faced outward as if encouraging her.

Hildegard Hopper's DeSoto pulled around the curve at the end of the yard and slid over the corner of Lolly's garden, crushing the tender trumpets of the petunias, the same kind of flower her mother had planted years ago and which Lolly tended lovingly. Hildegard continued on, apparently unaware of the damage she'd caused. Beside her in the front seat was perched her ever-present sidekick, Amelia Kramer.

"Oh, Lord, You'd better give me some patience and quick!" Lolly said aloud. "Don't let me say anything I'm going to regret later on."

She ran a hurried hand over her hair. As usual, she hadn't done much more than pull it back and wind it into a haphazard bun. It shouldn't matter that her hair wasn't as styled as theirs, she knew that, but there was just something about the way they acted that made her feel insecure.

She went to the door and pulled it open, a falsely hearty smile on her face, but they weren't there. They had, she realized, gone around the side of the house and were standing on each side of Colin.

The chickens had scattered to the far sides of the yard, but they were edging back closer. The two women were, after all, standing in the midst of their meal.

Lolly saw what was going to happen only seconds before it did. There was no time to stop it.

One chicken stepped over to Hildegard's right foot, stared at it for a moment, and then bobbed its head down and pecked at the glittery bow on the vamp. A plump hen gazed at her reflection in Amelia's shiny patent-leather sandals, and suddenly poked at it with her sharp beak.

The women's screams pierced the morning, and Lolly bit back a smile as she saw Colin trying to calm the women and the chickens. She rushed out and scooped up the two chickens and held them close to her as she tried to soothe them.

"Let me put them in the coop," she said over the loud protests of the chickens that wriggled fiercely in her arms, scratching her wrists and hands with their sharp claws. "I'll just be a moment. Colin, do you mind taking our guests inside and getting them settled while I see to things out here?"

He swept off the worn straw hat and bowed "I'd be delighted to. Ladies?" As he guided them into the house, she could hear him saying all the right things, tending to their own ruffled feathers.

She got the chickens settled and even gave them a little extra corn for their distress.

She could easily have stayed out there, relaxing under the

cottonwood and listening to the leaves. When she'd been little, she had thought the cottonwoods were whispering prayers when their leaves rustled in the faint breeze—and for just a moment she lingered in the shade.

But the thought of Colin at the mercy of Hildegard Hopper and Amelia Kramer brought her up sharply and she hurried back inside.

The two women were seated on either side of Colin, and the questions, in soft little voices with very pointed words, were flying at him like arrows.

"Where did you come from?"

"Do you have a family?"

"How long were you on the road?"

"What is your livelihood?"

"Will you stay here through winter?"

"Are you going back on the road?"

Motionless, he wasn't responding, which made their questioning even sharper.

"What are your plans?"

"Are you a Lutheran or a Baptist?"

"What was in your pack?"

"Do you miss your vagabond ways?"

She took immediate pity on him. "Hildegard, Amelia, can I get you something to drink? Tea perhaps? I'd offer you coffee, but we don't drink that in the summer. My brothers find it too heavy when it's this warm. I have some no-bake bars I made that I think you'll enjoy. I made them from a recipe I cut out a long time ago from the Mankato newspaper."

She knew she was chattering but she couldn't bear it anymore, seeing him beset by the barrage of questions.

They were, truth to tell, good questions, questions that needed answers, but he didn't need to share all that with the women. They were simply being nosy and meddlesome, always in search of a good juicy rumor to share at the store or after church.

Of course, what the women didn't know, and what Lolly and her brothers had managed thus far to avoid sharing with the townspeople, was that Colin didn't really know the answers himself, not entirely anyway. Every day his memory got stronger, and every day a bit more of it came back.

He didn't need to have these women assaulting him with a volley of questions.

Fortunately they were easy to deflect, and for the moment their mission was set aside, although she was sure that they would not let it go unsatisfied. What they didn't get today, they would return for another day. Hildegard and Amelia were relentless in their quest for gossip.

But temporarily at least, the onslaught was stilled, and the four of them sat in the stifling living room and made polite conversation about the cookery. None too soon the two women called an end to their visit, and with promises of recipes for blond brownies and oatmeal raisin bar cookies to be exchanged for copies of Lolly's newspaper clipping.

When Hildegard and Amelia were safely on the road again, Lolly collapsed in the chair by the couch. "I'm sorry you had to endure that," she said. "Those two are unbearable at times."

"I'm the one who should be apologizing," he said. "I feel like I'm taking advantage of you and your family."

Bruno's barking and a flurry of chicken squawks ended the somber discussion. The dog had figured out how to open the door to the coop and had apparently done it again. From the noise, Lolly was sure he'd gone inside to annoy the hens.

"I'll take care of it," he said, rising quickly. "He's all bark and no bite, but I'm afraid those chickens aren't quite as polite. I'd better save that mongrel before he meets the same fate as Hildegard's shoes."

She stayed in the chair and enjoyed the last minutes of solitude before mayhem broke loose. If the dog was back, so were her brothers, and they'd be hungry.

After they ate, maybe they'd all leave together. They'd started taking Colin with them out to the field and the barn, and she'd begun writing in her notebook again. After their meal, maybe she'd have the chance to put a few more words in it.

"Lolly!"

The door slammed open and then shut again as George and Bud burst into the room. Colin, she could see through the window, was still outside, kneeling in front of Bruno as the chickens watched curiously.

The dog had something in his mouth, as usual, and Colin was coaxing it out of his jaws.

Lolly rolled her eyes as she recognized the bow from Hildegard's shoe. First pecked by chickens and then chewed on by the dog, the ornament was beyond saving. Colin looked up, caught her watching from the window, and held up the trophy with a grin.

"Lolly, let's eat!" George, she could see, had already washed his hands and face at the pump—a layer of grime circled his hairline and his wrists where he hadn't washed. Well, she told herself, at least he had washed some of the dirt off.

"What are we having? Not that meat loaf again! What did you put in it? Gopher?" Bud grinned goofily as he slid into a chair at the kitchen table.

Bruno darted in front of Colin as he entered the house. Soon the small kitchen was filled with four people and a dog, and chaos ruled again.

&

The never-ending job of fence repair called the three men to the edge of the farmstead.

Colin rode along with the brothers. He'd elected to sit in

the back of the pickup truck with the dog rather than in the cab. It was hotter than an oven, but at least he got some air in his face, and he rather enjoyed bumping along the pitted road with Bruno for company.

Plus, riding in the back gave a fellow time to think about things that needed to be thought about. Like who he was.

Sure he knew his name was Colin Hammett. He'd led a life of comfort before this trip, but he only dimly remembered the details. His mind would find some piece of his former life, as he was calling it for lack of a better distinction, and sometimes the bit would take shape and become focused and grow, and he'd get another section of his past back.

Other times it was like trying to remember a dream. Details were slippery and would slither out of his reach when he'd try to grasp them.

He had so many questions. Why did he leave his life behind? He knew he had been well-off. The leather pack and the cashmere blankets he'd brought were proof of that. But why was he on the road? When he'd try to remember, his mind would almost let him get there, but it would stop just short of an answer.

Lolly and her brothers were terrific. They didn't push him but let him try to regain the lost ground on his own.

What an act of faith and trust that was! Could he have done the same, welcomed a stranger into his home as completely as they had?

The truck rumbled to a stop, and George and Bud got out.

"Fence work," George said. "Want to grab that toolbox, please?"

As far as Colin had been able to determine, fence posts worked themselves out of the ground at least once a week. They spent time every day riding the fence line and correcting the leaning posts, tightening wire where the fence was strung or replacing planks where the fence was lath.

"I don't know what we're keeping in," Bud grumbled as he wrestled with a post that refused to stay upright. "It's not like we have animals anymore, unless you count the chickens, and I don't know why you would."

"Eggs," George said around a mouthful of nails. "That's why Lolly keeps those nasty creatures around."

"Oh, they're not so bad," Colin said, trying to help Bud with the recalcitrant fence post. He told them the story of the chickens' reaction to the shoes worn by Hildegard and Amelia the day before. "I wouldn't be surprised if people all the way over in Minneapolis could have heard them, they were hollering so loud."

"I've just changed my opinion of chickens, then." Bud grinned at Colin.

"Bud," George chided, "watch what you say. Hildegard and Amelia have their good points. . .I'm sure."

They all laughed and returned to the business of fixing the fence.

His body was enjoying the labor. As the muscles flexed and tendons stretched, he felt better, and his recovery was speeding along. All that was left were a few missing pieces in his memory.

Sweat dripped off his chin. He leaned on the post while he swabbed it away with his handkerchief and took advantage of the respite to look around him.

This was beautiful country here. Admittedly the drought had taken its toll, but he could easily fill in the blanks and imagine the area with normal rain—and snow. The field was ringed with deep grasses that were looking somewhat parched at the moment, but he knew the trees, with deeper roots, had to be drawing water from the river to stay alive.

There was a metaphor somewhere in there but he was too

engaged in the scene to work it through. Maybe he'd figure it out later.

Yes, this place should be beautiful, come fall. He didn't know much about trees, but he did recognize the characteristic shape of the maple leaf, and he knew how extraordinary they were in autumn. Mingled in with the—

"Hey, dreamer," Bud said, giving him a light bop on the shoulder, "want to help me out? Here, dream on this post now."

Bud's grin told him that he was teasing, and as he headed to the next tilted fence post, the dog followed, settling at last in Colin's shadow.

George came over to fix the wire twisted around the post. "Look at you. Earlier this summer you wouldn't have held up a post. It would have held you up."

"Once it knocked me out," Colin joked. "It's amazing what food and water and a place to sleep can do for a body." He paused, wondering if he should read more into what George said. Was he implying that the time had come to move on?

It probably had, in all honesty. And the thought of leaving here brought immediate pain.

He'd come to love this family who'd taken him in so easily and so completely. Even the dog that lay drooling on the toe of his boot had worked his way into his heart.

Lolly, though—how that woman had put her imprint on his soul. A stray thought intruded—*maybe you're falling in love with her*—but he dismissed it. He'd known her less than three months, hardly long enough for that.

There had been an emptiness in him, though, that had started to fill in. And somehow that had to do with Lolly.

George rewound the wire. "Well, we're—oh, will you look at this?"

He bent over and ran his fingers over the post. "Someone's gone and carved something on it."

"Let me see." Bud pushed George aside and leaned in close. "Yup. Someone's carved a cat here."

"A cat? Now, why on earth would someone do that?" George stood up and dusted his hands off on the back of his overalls.

"Kind-hearted woman." Suddenly doors flew open and windows came unshuttered in Colin's mind. "Kind-hearted woman," he repeated. "That's what I saw. This was the spot!"

The brothers, he realized, were standing stock-still, staring at him as if he'd totally gone around the bend.

"It's the hobo sign. It means that a woman lives here who will feed you. A kind-hearted woman."

"Who? Lolly?" Bud chortled. "Lolly is a kind-hearted woman? You sure didn't grow up with her."

"I think she's a kind-hearted woman," Colin said.

George held up his hand. "Wait. Say that again."

"Say what?"

"She's a kind-hearted woman," Colin repeated.

"That's what he was saying," George said to his brother. "When we brought him into the house, and he kept saying something, and you, doofus, thought he was saying 'cigarette.'"

"Who's the doofus?" Bud shot back. "You thought he was asking for a cigar."

"A cigar? I don't smoke," Colin said.

"You weren't very clear when you first got to our house," George explained, "and we misunderstood what you said. Just forget that part. So you were really saying *kind-hearted woman*! I would never have guessed."

Bud snorted. "Especially if he had met Lolly. Her heart's made of stones and thistles and barbed wire."

George shushed him and as the two brothers joshed with each other, Colin thought of Lolly and smiled. *Kind-hearted woman, indeed!*

ða

That night, after the dishes were done and George and Bud were seated in front of the radio listening to the news, Colin and Lolly went for a walk. The sun was low but not set entirely.

"I want to show you something," Colin said to her, and he led her to the fence post with the carving on it. "This is where I hit my head."

She tilted her head in confusion. "Yes?"

"Look." He took her hand and traced the outline of the cat with the heart in it. "It's the kind-hearted woman sign."

"Who carved it? You?"

He laughed. "Lolly, if I'd carved it, you wouldn't be able to tell if it was a cat or an alligator. I don't know who carved it on here. Someone you'd helped before, I assume."

"Me?"

"Lolly, you're the kind-hearted woman. You're my kind-hearted woman."

ða

She wrote quickly, leaning over the kitchen counter next to the cake that had just come out of the oven, pouring the words of her imaginary love onto the paper. For some people, perhaps such love existed, but there was no place in her life for flowery phrases and romantic gestures. Yet in her notebook, with a flourish of her pencil, her life could change.

She began again to write the story she wanted to live.

As the letters fell onto the paper, the depression vanished. There was wealth in the land, waterfalls ran silver in the sunlight, flowers lifted sunny heads to the heavens and rejoiced.

And through it all she was happy.

Her hero had no name. Giving him a name would have grounded the dream, limited the scope so that it could never reach as far as it did now.

Her brothers would return soon, bringing both Colin and the dog with them, and her world would burst into crazed activity, with her brothers talking at the same time trying to tell her something they'd found that she probably didn't even care about, while Colin tried to help her finish supper preparations, and the dog ran in frantic circles around her feet on the off-chance she'd drop something edible.

Her heart flowed onto the page. Love lost, love found. It was the theme she knew really nothing about, but the drama appealed to the romantic in her.

There was a sound behind her, and she quickly closed the little book and stuffed it in her pocket.

"What are you doing?" Bud asked.

She shrugged. She couldn't lie, but on the other hand, she couldn't tell him the truth. He'd pester her forever.

"You were doing something."

"Don't be silly. I'm always doing something, you know that. Why, do you want to clean the counter for me? Is that what you're doing in here?" She'd learned a long time ago that the best way to get rid of her brothers was to ask them to do a household chore. They evaporated like water on a skillet in the face of a cleaning rag.

George and Colin were at the door. They had it half-cracked open, and the dog bounded in before she could stop him, a wriggling squirrel in his mouth. He dropped it cheerfully at her feet and chased it around the kitchen, barking as it climbed the Hoosier cabinet, leaped across to the curtains and pulled them down rod and all, ran over the counter, through the cake she'd set out to cool, and down the hall to the bedrooms.

"Bruno!" they shouted in unison. And while she tried to get Bruno out of the house—which he did not want to do, not with a squirrel running loose in the house, a squirrel that he had caught himself, no less—the men tried to shoo the equally excited animal out.

At last the squirrel had been rescued and released, the dog had been pacified with a beef bone, and Lolly slumped as she looked at the cake. The top of it had been torn apart when the squirrel had raced across it, and crumbs littered the countertop. No one could eat it now. She sighed and scraped it into the dog's dish.

Where was her hero when she needed him the most?

five

*The forest is fragranced with green. Deep moss cushions
our path, and each footstep releases lush, woodsy aromas
that surround us. The trees are in the height of summer
glory, each leaf displaying its own variant of green. From
the jeweled shrubbery of emerald and jade to the graying
patina of lichen on the tree trunks to the dazzling brilliance
of bright green grass in a patch of sun through the canopy,
we are blessed by the richness of the day, we two, who stroll
hand in hand.*

August seemed to fly by on winged feet. Each sunlit hour
passed entirely too quickly as summer breathed its most fiery
breaths in the grand finale of the season.

Every day Colin got stronger, and every day Lolly became
more attached to him. From being able to reach the bread
plate on the highest cupboard shelf to holding the outside
washbasin when she needed to empty it, he had become an
integral part of her life.

The question that was never answered—because it was
never asked—was what would happen in the future. Would he
stay on with them? As much as she'd enjoy having him around,
their lives couldn't stay this way forever. He was living in the
old house, a temporary arrangement at best, but it was only a
matter of time before the tongues in town would begin to wag,
with Hildegard and Amelia leading the way.

And if he chose to leave? That was the worst outcome
possible. Where would he go? Back on the road? Living from

town to town, shivering his way across a wintry America in search of—in search of what?

She couldn't bear the thought of him leaving and going back to living as a vagabond. He was flourishing with them. Alone—why, who knew where that lifestyle could lead him?

Would he have a safe place to lay his head at night? Would he have enough to eat? Would he be safe?

Would he miss her?

She cut the thought before it went any further. It wasn't productive, and it could only make her sad. What she needed to do today was go into town and do some shopping. George told her the evening before that Martin Jorgens, the grocer, had asked him if she had any eggs she could sell him. He'd run short.

One thing her chickens did was lay eggs, and lots of them. She'd gathered them in a basket lined with a kitchen towel, and asked George to drive her to town.

Colin and Bud were out in the back with Bruno, ostensibly planning a toolshed near the chicken coop, but she was sure they probably were just talking. There was no reason to interrupt them. Plus it was always simply easier to leave someone at home, or else Bruno would chase after the truck until one of her brothers took pity on him and let him ride in the bed of the truck—and then they had the dog to contend with for the rest of the day.

It wasn't going to be a long trip to town anyway. The eggs had to be delivered quickly, since in this heat they'd run the risk of spoiling. She'd do that first, and then stop at the drugstore to get some aspirin.

The trip to town was pleasant. George wasn't a big talker, so Lolly was able to roll the window down, lean her head out, and let the air blow on her face and just relax.

"You look just like Bruno right now," George said.

Lolly pulled her head back into the cab of the truck. "I do not."

"Well, okay, you're not drooling and you haven't barked at any squirrels, but you have the same blissful expression on your face that he does when he sticks his head out the window."

She laughed. "It does feel wonderful, George, and you should probably try it—sometime when you're not driving, of course. Especially when it's this hot, the wind on my face feels great." She had a sudden terrible thought. "Be honest. Does my hair look all right?"

He snorted. "As much as it ever does."

Trust a brother not to give an answer that told her anything. She tried to check her reflection in the mirror he had rigged up after nearly backing up over the minister one time, but he kept swatting her away. "You're going to make me drive off the road here. Hey, you're sticking your elbow in my ear. Ow! Stop it! Your hair's fine. It's growing on your head, it's not purple, what more do you want?"

"Forget it," she answered. He'd never understand.

"I'll be at Ruth's having a cola," he said. "Meet me there when you're through."

She suppressed a smile. Her brother spent a lot of time at Ruth's Café, most of it talking to Ruth. He could make a single cola last for hours if necessary, although she suspected that Ruth would freshen it as necessary to keep him here.

She waited until he'd parked the truck along the main street before giving her appearance a quick check. No one would ever beg to paint her portrait, but she was presentable.

With her basket of eggs balanced carefully on her arm, she entered the grocery store. The market wasn't crowded at all. Two women paused at the fruit and vegetable counter and casually examined the celery while chattering away.

Martin Jorgens greeted her. "Oh, Lolly, I'm so glad you're here. I'm down to the last egg. I hope you brought me at least a dozen."

"Two dozen, if that's all right."

She put the basket on the counter and carefully unfolded the towel that was tucked around the precious cargo. "They all look whole."

"Lucky, knowing the way George drives," Martin answered, and they both laughed. George was probably the most sedate driver in Valley Junction. She could probably have put the eggs on the hood of the truck while they rode into town, and the eggs would still be intact.

The women had stopped talking and looked over at her. She recognized them as wives of farmers on the northeast side of town. She didn't know them well, but she smiled and nodded at them. "Think it'll cool off ever?"

The women smiled back and one of them said, "I would hope so. Cooling off would do everyone good, I think," and the other woman laughed before turning her attention to a packet of carrots and saying something under her breath to her companion.

Lolly felt the blood rush to her face. She had no idea what prompted this from these women that she barely knew, but the condescension was obvious.

What could have brought this on? She checked to make sure the hem of her dress wasn't tucked up behind her and that her shoes matched.

The two women put their heads together and made a great act of pretending to discuss the carrots, but their gazes flitted back to Lolly and they snickered.

Then they laid down the carrots, and both women left together, still smiling over some shared secret.

Martin shook his head. "Biddies," he muttered as he took

the eggs from the basket. "I'm surprised they don't cackle and lay their own eggs. Come in here every time their husbands visit town, and I've yet to sell them a thing. Apparently my products aren't as highfalutin as what they'd get in Mankato."

Lolly frowned. "I thought they were talking about me."

"Probably were," he said almost cheerfully. "Those two are the kind that aren't happy unless they have someone else's arm to chew on. Don't waste any time on them. They sure won't waste any on you, unless it's to find something to talk about."

"But that's hardly reassuring," she answered.

He shrugged. "Lolly, they will talk about you, I can guarantee that. They'll talk about me. They'll talk about Ruth over at the café, and Joe at the drugstore. If they see the minister, they'll talk about him, and if they don't see him, they'll still talk about him."

She laughed. "Point taken."

"Why some people have to be that way is beyond me. I figure I have enough to do chasing after my own life without getting that picky about everybody else's life, too. You know, if we all took a page from the Good Book and do unto others, the world would be a right friendlier place."

"Martin, I feel a lot better!"

She was much happier when she left, the coins from the sale of the eggs jingling in her dress pocket. When she got home, she'd put some aside and drop them into the glass jar she had hidden in the back of her closet. It wasn't the most original place to hide it, but her brothers weren't the most original thinkers, so she figured the money was safe.

What she was going to do with it, she had no idea, although the thought of a trip to Paris was lovely. At the rate she was going, she'd have enough saved to go by the time she was two hundred and three.

Her next stop was the drugstore. It was, as always, dark and fragrant with the scent of wintergreen and licorice and alcohol.

Joe Albee called a hello as she walked to the counter. The floor of the pharmacy was made of wide wooden planks and they creaked loudly under her feet. It was all part of the charm of the drugstore.

"What can I get you, Lolly?" he asked.

"Just a box of aspirin today," she answered.

"Those brothers of yours giving you a headache, are they?" He chuckled as he retrieved the aspirin for her.

"They wouldn't be my brothers if they weren't."

"Those two can do some pretty crazy things, that's for sure." He handed her the aspirin. "Here you go. Now, you try not to overheat, you hear me?"

She was probably reading too much into innocent conversations, she told herself as she walked toward the café. It was August after all, and it was hot, and people were trying to cool off.

If only she had her notebook with her! This would translate well into the emerging story she was writing. As soon as she got home, she would steal a few minutes away and write this part of the tale.

She strolled to the café, taking her time as she spun the story out in her mind. She was in no hurry. George always dallied at the café to talk to Ruth, and although he might bark at her about how slow she was, she knew he truly didn't mind.

Maybe she could take some time to window-shop.

The display at Leubner's Store featured a woman's dress in a raucous pattern of yellow and red swirls. Just looking at it made Lolly dizzy. A brooch thick with faux gems caught the matching scarf flung dramatically over one shoulder.

It was undoubtedly out of the price range of most women in Valley Junction, but she knew what would happen.

The dress was one of a kind, the sign below it boasted. The designer's name wasn't one she'd heard of, but that didn't mean much. She wasn't up on the current fashion scene.

She had time, she realized, to step into Leubner's and see what the styles were. She made her own dresses, but maybe she could get a few ideas for updating her patterns.

The rotating blades on the ceiling moved the air in the store, but failed to cool it. A young woman stood behind the counter, a Chinese paper fan languidly waving in her hand.

"Afternoon!" she called. She was the daughter of the teacher in Valley Junction, a pretty young woman with elegantly straight hair as black as a raven's wing. She was in Bud's class at school, and had always struck Lolly as someone who seemed much older than she undoubtedly was.

"Good afternoon," Lolly replied.

"Can I show you something?"

"Well, I have to admit that I was drawn in by the dress in the window."

The young woman nodded. "It's already sold. But you can take a look at it if you want."

"Thanks, but it's not quite my style."

The clerk laughed. "It's almost no one's style."

Lolly didn't need to ask who had bought it, or why it was still on display if it had been sold, or what the sales clerk's comment meant.

The dress on the mannequin was very small. Only a tiny, quite petite woman could wear it.

But in two or three weeks, the dress, Lolly knew, would vanish from the store window and appear on the body of Hildegard Hopper.

The purpose of this artfully engineered ruse was common

knowledge in Valley Junction. Hildegard had created it herself.

She had Leubner's send away for the dress in her size, and when it arrived, the smaller version would disappear. Hildegard had made the slight mistake of confiding her reasoning to one of the store's earlier and chattier clerks, who had almost immediately left the employ of Leubner's once the story escaped into the fast-moving environment of Valley Junction's rumor mill.

Hildegard's reasoning behind the scheme was this: People would think that Hildegard was wearing the smaller dress, and they would see her, then, as a less formidably sized woman.

The plan, of course, never worked, but no one dared tell Hildegard, and Lolly had to admit that the town took a very wrong pleasure in being in on the rather twisted workings of Hildegard Hopper's mind.

"Would you like to try something on?" the clerk asked. "You know that the trend now is neckline accents." She came from behind the counter and pulled out a green dress with white rickrack edging and an oversized flounce that surrounded the shoulders like a cape. "This, for example, is quite lovely. Look at the detail!"

Lolly glanced at the dress and ran her hand over the offerings in her size. None of them appealed to her.

"I'm not much on big bows and floppy collars," she confessed. "When I've tried to wear them, I feel like something isn't zipped or buttoned or tied."

The young woman laughed. She hung the dress up again and returned to her spot behind the counter. "I understand that. Say, can I ask you—are you Lolly Prescott?"

"I am."

"My name is Sarah Fallon. My mother was Bud's teacher a couple of years ago."

"I thought I recognized you. Please extend my sympathies to your mother; I can imagine Bud wasn't the most thoughtful student." Lolly abandoned the dresses with a sigh.

Sarah chuckled. "I liked him. We had some classes together this year. He adds energy to the class."

"That's one way to put it."

The clerk made a great show of wiping off the counter. "Is Bud seeing anyone?"

Lolly stopped. Could she be hearing this right? "Bud? My brother?"

She'd never thought of Bud in this context before, and definitely not with someone as stylish as Sarah. Lolly's mind tried to put her wild brother with this fashionable young lady, and failed.

Sarah continued to focus on the glass surface of the counter. "Bud makes me laugh. I like that. We're not exactly Jean Harlow and Clark Gable, but I don't think that matters."

Lolly laughed. "Him as Clark Gable? Never. Maybe one of the Marx brothers, though." She sorted through the jewelry display on the counter as she considered the idea of her brother as a matinee idol.

"So nobody can really blame you for what you did." Sarah smiled a bit awkwardly.

Lolly stopped investigating the necklaces and bracelets. "What I did? What did I do?"

Sarah shook her head. Her hands fluttered like dragonflies as she dismissed her own words. "Nothing. Just that you have that handsome man with you—what's his name?"

"Colin, and he's not my handsome anything. Well, he is handsome, but he's not mine." Lolly quit while what she said still made some sense. This was a conversation headed down a bad road. It was best to end it quickly.

The young woman smiled. "I understand. I sure don't

blame you. We do what we need to, don't we?"

A customer entered the store, and Lolly fled, grateful for the interruption. She wasn't sure she wanted to hear what the young woman thought she'd done. This had all the markings of the gossip-mouths in town, two of them in particular.

She wanted to hurry home, back to the security of the farm—back to her trying brothers, a mysterious guest, an always-hungry dog, and chickens that attacked women's shoes. *That* was normal.

As she walked to the café, she focused on the idea of Bud and Sarah. Should she say anything to him? The temptation to rag him about it was nearly overwhelming, but she fought it. Maybe the best idea was to keep it to herself. Telling Bud about it would doom the relationship immediately. He'd undoubtedly do something like get gum stuck in that lovely hair. And if George got wind of it, he'd never let the subject die.

No, the best thing was to keep it to herself. Sometimes the young woman came to church. Maybe she could play matchmaker a bit.

The café was vacant, except for Ruth and George, and Ruth slid a cola down the counter to her with a practiced hand. "Here, honey," Ruth said. "Cool yourself down."

George shot the young woman a look that Lolly couldn't quite read, and he pushed his chair back suddenly.

Ruth flushed an immediate brick red. "I didn't mean—" she said, as the crimson deepened. "I meant—oh, you know I'd never—well, it's August—but not that—"

"Let's go," he said abruptly to Lolly. "I've got work to do."

"Can I at least have my drink?"

"No." George slammed a nickel on the counter. "Keep the change," he muttered.

"There's no change," Lolly began, but he pulled her by the elbow out of the café, without even a good-bye to Ruth.

When they were in the truck again, she turned to face her brother. "Well, that was rude," she said. "Is something wrong between you and Ruth? Did I walk into the middle of an argument?"

He didn't answer for a while, and then he simply said, "I'm taking you home."

He was silent the entire ride home, and Lolly chewed on her lip nervously.

This didn't bode well at all.

six

Ahead of us there is a bridge. Under the slatted wood, water ripples over moss-covered rocks that line the river's edge and continue beneath the liquid surface. Trees arch overhead, shading us as we step onto the bridge. The planks creak as we pass over the bridge, but we hold onto each other's hands and tread carefully. The bridge sways, but still we know the alternative is to wade across the river—and we have no idea how deep the water is, how slick the moss is, and how sharp the stones are. "Take my hand," he invites. "Trust me."

Colin sat at the table, peeling potatoes for her. She'd tried to tell him that he didn't have to, but the repetitive motion was pleasant. After being on the road and then struggling to recover from acute memory loss, he was enjoying the experience of something as everyday as peeling potatoes.

Lolly's brothers were out at the shed. George had asked Colin to give him some time to talk to Bud alone, and Colin was glad to oblige.

Plus, he liked being around Lolly. She didn't have Bud's unbridled wildness or George's stodginess. Instead, she was calm and funny and capable. Lolly was the anchor in the family, although he was sure the brothers didn't recognize that.

He dropped a curl of potato skin and Bruno snapped it up.

Bit by bit his memory was returning. There were only a few gaps in it, and he sometimes wondered if they were there because he didn't want to remember it all.

He knew, for example, that he wasn't married. He did know that he had been employed in the publishing and printing business in New York City, although he was vague on the details. He had some remembrance of setting out on the road—and a man and a Bible verse that he only partially remembered but which Lolly'd helped him put together again. *Blessed is the man that trusteth in the Lord.*

Did he trust in the Lord? It was a question that gnawed him, especially at bedtime, when his head was on the pillow but sleep was elusive in the August-hot night. He worried about himself and God. He longed for that same trust Lolly had, that God was in control, that He hadn't forgotten this depression-ridden country, that prosperity would return, if not in the form of material riches, then as a wealth of the spirit.

He could remember, now with startling clarity, the church he'd attended in New York City; and although his brain tried to block the images, he also remembered his pride, his *hubris*, as it was called, in how devout he was.

But now he knew that this had been only a surface faith, that he'd never truly taken the Bible completely to his heart.

So he read the Bible the man had given him not so long ago, and each time he found himself edging closer to understanding it, but he couldn't yet make the leap from knowing it to believing it. His head ached some nights trying to determine why he couldn't simply have a faith like Lolly's.

Here he'd thought he was the perfect Christian, and she'd shown him there was much more to it.

"Penny for your thoughts." Lolly's voice interrupted his musing.

He laughed. "That's about what they're worth."

"You looked so serious sitting there."

He could hear the concern rising in her voice. "Peeling

potatoes is serious business," he answered lightly, hoping to allay her anxiety. "Are those carrots ready yet? I think it's about time to add them to the pot. Let me finish this spud. Is this about the right size you want them cut to?"

He continued to talk as he scooped up the potatoes and carried them to the large stewpot, in which meat cubes bubbled in a savory gravy. "Sure smells good," he said.

She moved aside to let him slide the potatoes in while she continued to stir. Today her hair was tied back with a red ribbon, limp from her work at the stove.

As they stood shoulder to shoulder at the stove, billows of pungent steam wrapped around them.

"You know, this is better than the most costly French perfume," he declared. "Actually, if Chanel had thought of it, she'd have bottled it."

On a whim, he seized her by the waist and whirled her around, setting her squarely in the middle of the room. "Lolly, let's capture this in a bottle, and we'll sell it and be millionaires! We'll travel to the south of France, and be the toast of Paris society, and we'll eat oysters and lobsters and steaks every day, served to us on the finest bone china. For dessert, we'll dip strawberries in chocolate and eat truffles with our fingers. What do you say? Shall we?"

Her face was only inches from his, and for a moment neither one of them spoke.

He realized, with some surprise, that it would be so easy to bridge that gap, put his lips on hers—and that he wanted to. But those inches might as well have been miles. He couldn't do that. He wouldn't do that, not until he knew her heart.

Plus, it wouldn't be right, not with him still living here.

He pulled his hands away from her waist and laughed, a bit rockily. "Maybe not. Somehow I don't think Eau de Beef Stew would be quite as popular as Chanel No. 5."

She smoothed the front of her apron. "Well," she said, "I suppose—"

Her words were cut short by a shrill "Yoo-hoo" from the open front door. The sound carried to the kitchen like a rusty saw on metal.

"Oh, no. Please, no," she said under her breath. But he noticed that she had managed to create a smile as she walked to the door.

"We can tell that you're getting ready to eat," Hildegard began, and Colin forced himself not to roll his eyes. Why on earth would they come by at this time of day? Didn't they know that most people were getting ready to eat? In order for them to skip dinner, he realized, they must be on the trail of something more delicious than Lolly's stew.

"Yes, indeed, I'll be serving very soon," Lolly answered.

"What are you making for dinner?" Hildegard asked, sniffing the air and looking for all the world like Bruno, who sat at attention near Colin's feet, his snout poked upward and quivering in delight at the aromas swirling around him.

"Nothing more exciting than stew," Lolly said.

"You know, we heard the most interesting story today," Hildegard burbled. "Didn't we, Amelia?"

Her sidekick nodded enthusiastically. "Yes, we did. Very interesting, indeed."

"That's quite intriguing, and I'm sure we'd love to hear it, but—"

"Oh, you would enjoy this story, I'm sure of that. Wouldn't they enjoy it, Amelia?"

"Both of them would," Amelia agreed.

"Well, it will have to wait for another time, I'm sorry to say, unless of course—"

Colin's hands cramped from the fists he made. Certainly Lolly would invite them, out of politeness. They couldn't accept, could they?

They couldn't, Hildegard explained. They were just out for a drive and thought they'd stop by and say hello. But since they'd obviously caught Lolly and Colin at a bad time, they'd visit another time.

Don't turn around and look at me, Colin said to Lolly silently. *Don't give them the satisfaction.*

Lolly kept her composure and within seconds the women were on their way to Hildegard's DeSoto.

Colin smiled as Lolly adroitly maneuvered the two women into the car. She was quite a woman. If it had been up to him, he would have ushered them right out the back door, into the unwelcoming midst of the chickens.

"You know what they're doing, don't you?" Lolly said as she stared after the car. "They saw us, and they'll make the most of it."

"They saw nothing," he said with a confidence he didn't feel. "How could they have seen anything? We were in the kitchen. Plus, it's not like we were doing anything scandalous. If they had seen anything, it would have been nothing more than two friends who care for each other very much. What's newsworthy about that?"

She glanced at him over her shoulder. "In their hands, nothing becomes something very quickly."

"Perhaps."

"I wonder what the story was that they were talking about." She frowned. "Today in town, people were acting really odd."

"Here? In Valley Junction?" He laughed.

"I'm sure it's just another of their tales, something little that they've made into national news. Call FDR himself, and have him put it in one of his Fireside Chats. Lolly, I suspect that almost everybody in Valley Junction knows what they're like, that their stories can't be trusted. I wouldn't worry. Maybe you could enjoy the notoriety, which I suspect will be short-lived without verification from another source."

She laughed. "I could enjoy notoriety? What a thought! Meanwhile, go get my brothers and tell them to get ready for supper. And tell them that their sister is notorious. They'll like that."

George and Bud were pulling down an old storage hut that had seen better days, with the plan that the wood could be used for other projects. Already a neat stack of boards was placed beside the partially razed lean-to.

Bruno accompanied Colin, staying close at his heels until he saw a butterfly that he chased and amazingly caught— and ate. That dog was an omnivore, for sure. There wasn't anything he wouldn't eat.

As Colin got nearer, he could hear George and Bud's words clearly.

"Bud, you shouldn't have done that. Ruth told me. The story had already gotten over to her."

"It was funny. You've got to give me that. I mean, *jeweled shrubbery*? When was the last time you saw a bush with diamonds hanging on it? You show it to me, because I'm tired of being poor. Let's harvest those diamonds!"

"Funny for you. Not funny for Lolly." George pounded a board free. "You have to think before you speak, little brother. This is really going to hurt her."

Colin's stomach tightened. This didn't sound at all good. He stepped behind the barn, just out of their direct sight, but where he could see and hear them. He didn't want to eavesdrop, but this didn't seem to be a conversation he could rightfully interrupt.

"Nah, she's a tough one. She'll be mad at me but she'll get over it, eventually. She's no little delicate flower waiting for her prince to come riding in." Bud snorted.

"She isn't? You read it. You know what she wrote. Put one and one together and see if you don't get two." George glared at his brother.

"Why wouldn't I get two? What do you get when you add one and one?"

George shook his head. "Honestly, some days I just don't know about you. I think you're putting one and one together and getting one and a half."

Bud stood up. "You're talking in riddles."

"I'm talking the truth here, Bud. You have to tell her."

"I don't want to." Bud kicked one of the loose boards, and the tidy pile fell apart. "She's going to be mad."

"You can be sure of that. Tonight, after dinner, you have to tell her what you did," George announced. "It's the right thing to do."

"You mean it's the scary thing to do. She's going to kill me."

"If you're lucky. If you're not lucky, she'll let you live and she'll make you suffer for a long, long time. Deservedly so, I might add." George began rebuilding the stack of boards. "You're going to be in big trouble, brother. Big trouble."

Colin coughed and crashed against the side of the barn, just to make noise to let them know he was near. Bruno, having finished eating the butterfly, stopped to bite off a dandelion and swallow it.

"Dinnertime," Colin called to the brothers. "Lolly made stew."

"I don't want to go," Bud began, but his brother grabbed him by the elbow and led him toward Colin, saying something that Colin couldn't make out. But by the set of George's jaw, he could guess the gist of it.

This was going to be an interesting night.

❧

"That was excellent stew, dearest sister," Bud said after dinner. "Now I think I will end the meal with a nice stroll outside."

"Not so fast," George said. "Lolly, leave the bowls. Bud has something he wants to tell you."

"I can listen and start the dishes at the same time," she said. "You know I don't like to let them sit and get crusty. They're harder to wash that way."

"I suspect that you shouldn't have anything in your hands when you hear what Bud has to tell you. Bud, tell her. Now." George leaned back and crossed his arms over his chest.

Colin stood up and carried his dish to the sink. "I have the feeling that this is a family-only conversation, and I think I'll leave the three of you to sort it out."

"Do you know what's going on?" She took the bowl from him and rinsed it in the sink.

"No, I don't, and I undoubtedly don't need to know. I'll just head out and read for a while."

He left the kitchen, and when the screen door slammed and the sound of his whistling his way across the yard to the old house carried over the night air and through the open windows, she turned to her brothers.

"I don't want to hear this, do I?" she asked, as a feeling of dread clutched her stomach.

"No, you don't," Bud said, standing up and stretching, "which is why I'm going to take that walk."

"Sit." George seized Bud's belt and pulled his brother back into his chair. "Talk."

"Do I have to?" Bud wheedled. "I don't want to ruin a perfectly good dinner and a perfectly good evening with a perfectly horrible story."

"Ruin it." George glared at him.

"Well," Bud began, "it all started when I needed a blanket."

"A blanket? In this weather?" Lolly frowned at her brother. Had he totally lost his mind?

"*I* didn't need a blanket. But Floyd did."

"Floyd. Ah. That explains it. Who's Floyd?" This conversation was getting weirder by the minute, and from the grim expression on George's face and the worry on Bud's, she knew it wasn't going to get better.

"Floyd B. Olson."

"The governor of Minnesota needed a blanket from us?" Lolly put her face in her hands. This had to be a dream.

"No, silly. Floyd is the new rooster." Bud picked up a leftover roll and began to shred it.

"You named the rooster after the governor? Why would you do that?" she asked from between her fingers.

"Well, it would have been impolite to name him after the president. So I couldn't call him Franklin."

"Of course not." She had a terrible urge to laugh, but she didn't dare. This conversation was not headed in a humorous direction.

"Get on with the story," George growled.

"All right. I wanted a blanket for Floyd. He'd had a bit of a run-in with the old rooster, and he had a big scratch on his—"

"Bud!" George's voice was stern. "Watch it!"

"Well," Bud continued, his fingers still toying with the roll, "Floyd wouldn't be too comfortable sitting on the straw, so I had to get him something softer, and I knew there was one in your bedroom closet, and—"

She knew where this was going.

She flew out of her chair. "You did *not*! Tell me now that you did not read it!"

Bud made dough balls out of the now-destroyed roll. "Sure, I'll tell you that. I didn't read it."

"Bud," George growled warningly, "you can't run from this."

Her younger brother looked down and crumpled the rest of the roll. "Well, maybe I did."

She wanted to cry. Her beautiful dream story. Her escape

from the financial mess the country was in and this hot, hot farm. Her window, however imaginary, out of a life that offered her no choices, no chances. It was gone, all gone.

Her brother had taken the beauty from her life as surely as if he'd gone after it with scissors and knives.

She took off her apron and then put it back on again. Everything was so mixed up now. She began to gather the remaining dishes from the table, so calm that it seemed as if something had died inside of her. Her life was flat. "I give up."

"Lolly, no." George's forehead crinkled.

"Well, why shouldn't I? I tried one little thing, one tiny little nothing thing. It didn't hurt anyone. It didn't do anything. But now, it's been taken from me."

"You can have it back," he said. "I put it in your room this afternoon."

"You don't get it, do you?" She leaned across the table, picking up the empty stew tureen and cradling it to her chest.

She sank back into her chair, putting the tureen in front of her. "That notebook was mine. Mine. It was the only thing I have that was mine. And now, you've destroyed it."

"I'm sorry, Lolly."

She didn't say anything. Her beautiful story, her one shining bit of beauty that she had created, was now tarnished. The anger that boiled inside her began to mourn the loss of her privacy. But Bud looked so miserable her heart began to relent. "I guess it could be worse," she said at last.

George touched her hand. "Sis, it can. Bud, finish the story."

"She's not near any knives, is she?" Bud asked.

"Not funny. Finish the story." George wrapped his hand around hers. "Lolly, in advance, I'm sorry. You did not deserve this."

The room was silent until at last Bud put the remaining bits of the roll down and stared at the crumbs.

"I told some people, and some other people were there, and I think they told some other people."

Lolly didn't need for him to tell her who they were. She already knew. She could sense the hands of Hildegard Hopper and Amelia Kramer in this.

God, this would be a good time to take me Home.

"I need to leave," she said. "Please excuse me."

George tightened his grip on her hand. "I hate to tell you this, but there's more. Bud, please continue."

"I might have sort of led these people to think that maybe there could be, well—I implied a little bit that Colin is your mail-order groom."

seven

*The river twists and turns back onto itself, a golden ribbon
in the fading summer sun. Soon the trees will be bare, and
the leaves will float down the river, away from where they
began and flourished. Winter's hoary head will claim even
the river, then. He holds my hand one last time and promises
me that tomorrow the sun will shine, the stars will twinkle,
and the moon will glow. But we will not be together.*

Lolly sat on her bed. All the lights were extinguished, and
she sat in the darkness and talked to God.

*We've been through a lot together, You and I, and I've trusted You—
and I still do. I don't understand why things happen the way they
do. My parents should have lived longer. I miss them so much. Every
day is a struggle to keep the family together. And now, this. I'm not
asking You to explain it to me—although if You'd like to, I'm willing to
listen—but I would like some guidance here. What do I do?*

In the clear night, she could hear a dog barking from a
neighboring farmstead, and Bruno's baying response. Beyond
them, another dog howled. They were just like the rumor
network in Valley Junction, she thought. From one dog to
another, the story got spread.

Mail-order groom!

She hadn't been able to look at her brothers after Bud had
told her the horrible news. She hadn't even done the dishes,
but she'd heard her brothers in the kitchen taking care of
cleaning up. Tomorrow she'd probably have to redo the
dishes, or, she thought with some meanness, she could make

Bud eat out of the dirty ones.

Had they said anything to Colin? What was his reaction? She groaned as she realized that not only did she have the townspeople to deal with, she had him, too.

Mail-order groom!

What had she said in the notebook that had led to it? Anything? Or had it been all Bud's overactive imagination?

She stood up and crossed the room to check in her closet. In the dark, she felt around the top shelf where the blanket had been, and her fingers found nothing.

The notebook was missing, but at this stage, it was all water under the bridge or whatever the appropriate metaphor was.

The notebook was gone, and with it, her reputation.

No wonder the women at the grocery store had been eyeing her with amusement. The druggist. The clerk at the clothing store. Even Ruth. To them she was a woman so desperate for love that she'd sent for a man to marry!

Hildegard and Amelia had probably taken the story and embroidered it even more. She didn't want to think what they might have done with it.

But her mind wouldn't let the fact rest and batted it around fruitlessly, like a cat playing with a toy mouse. A mail-order groom!

Her own brother had told the story, too, lending a great degree of credibility to it. So even if Colin were right, when he'd said earlier that the people of Valley Junction would simply dismiss Hildegard and Amelia's story as silly gossip, it circled back to that. Bud had started the story.

Plus, what would Colin think of the story? It would probably drive him out of town, away from her forever. She thought of Colin at the stewpot, then twirling her around with the lure of Eau de Beef Stew making them rich.

It was silly, so silly that it made her laugh through her heartache. Eau de Beef Stew!

They'd stood together, right there in the kitchen, his arms around her waist. She'd thought he was going to kiss her.

Even now, reliving it, she was amazed at how much she wanted him to.

She'd gone all these years without being kissed, except, of course, by her parents, and that one time behind the school when she was thirteen. It had been a quick, experimental peck on the cheek, given by a boy who had long ago moved away from Valley Junction, and whose name she'd forgotten.

But a real kiss—that was the stuff that she'd never let herself even dream of, except in her notebook. And at that moment in the kitchen, it had seemed like her creation and real life might actually meet.

No. It hadn't happened, and that told her everything. They had both been caught up in the moment—a dangerous thing, that—and it was better that it hadn't gone further.

Still, Eau de Beef Stew. It made her smile.

But like a drumbeat of a dirge, under the memory was this new twist, and it stripped away all of the sweetness and replaced it with a sour, spoiled taste.

She'd come so close to love, so close, and now it was slipping out of her grasp.

❧

Colin had spent most of the night awake, trying to first of all, figure out what had happened, and second, how to deal with it. George had filled him in, feeling that it was only fair that he was aware what the situation was.

Here he'd worried about being a burden on the family economically, but this came out of nowhere and caught him off guard. Now his very presence had put Lolly in a socially precarious spot.

He was angry at Bud. Angry that he'd put Lolly in this position, angry he'd put him in it. Bud's impulsiveness was part of his charm, but there was nothing charming about what he had done.

Through the dark hours he'd tossed and turned, searching for a cool spot in the August heat and talking alternately to himself and to God.

He still wasn't totally accustomed to being this familiar with God—he was used to the formal tone of his church in the city, where the language of prayer employed *Thou* and *Thee* and, of course, *hast* and *shalt*. His time with the Prescott family, however, had made God more real to him, and he knew that no matter what words he used, God understood him, even if he didn't totally understand God.

It wasn't one of those electric moments, when the light came on and all things spiritual were clear. That would be nice, he had to acknowledge, but it didn't happen that way.

Instead, bit by bit he began to move, to edge, to creep into the light of the truth. And always, God was there, listening to him. Now it was time to listen to God.

The situation with Bud was dire. What was he to do about it? Something? Anything? Nothing?

Forgive. That was the only solution he could come up with, and it wasn't going to be easy. These wounds cut deep.

Forgiving seemed a lot easier in principle than it was in action. Bud was the kind of person who bumbled and blurted his way through life, and Colin was sure this wasn't the first time he'd done something hurtful to his family. But this one was possibly the most virulent blunder he'd made.

Maybe the best idea wasn't to forgive Bud, at least not right away. He certainly needed to understand how much his actions had hurt his sister. Bud needed to squirm under the hot light of his own shame.

Even as he thought it, he realized the herculean task ahead of him.

It was easy to be the forgiven one, but much more difficult to be the forgiver.

How do You do it, God? How do You forgive, and yet lead us to know better?

He turned the question around in his mind, but still it made no more sense than it had initially.

The sun had begun its rosy climb over the horizon before he'd finally drifted off into an exhausted but fretful sleep.

Breakfast was a somber meal, with all of them eating in silence. Colin furtively watched the siblings as they bent over their food. No one really ate anything, and clearly appetites had suffered after the prior evening's disclosure.

Bud finally burst out, "All right! I am horrible! I am terrible! Hate me! I deserve it!" and ran from the kitchen.

Lolly moved as if to follow after him, but George stopped her. "Let him go."

"George, did you hear what he said? I can't let him—"

"Lolly, you have to let him feel the wrong. If you don't, he'll find a way to justify it, and he won't have learned anything. He'd probably do it again."

She sighed and rubbed her forehead. "This isn't easy," she said. "I don't know what to do."

If only life were written in pencil, Colin thought, he could take an eraser and undo all the missteps.

"George," she said to him, "there's something else. The notebook isn't in my room. He said he put it in there, but it's not on the shelf and not on my dresser."

"You know how he is," her brother said. "He gets mentally waylaid easily. He must have meant to put it in there, but I saw it on the floor next to his hat. And yes, I know his hat isn't supposed to be on the floor, and that's how I saw the notebook, when I was picking up his hat. I put it in your room on the chair."

"It wasn't there. You don't suppose he took it again, do you? Did he have it with him when he went to town?"

George grimaced. "He had it, of course. He, well, Lolly, he read some of it out loud in the bank."

She put her face in her hands and groaned.

"But he brought it home. That's when I saw it. It's here somewhere. You'll find it. Maybe you just picked it up without realizing it."

Lolly shrugged, and Colin's heart twisted at the hopelessness in the gesture. "It doesn't matter. What's done is done."

He started to move toward her, but George interrupted him.

"Colin, let's go work on that shed. I'd like to have it finished by supper." George stood up, and Colin followed suit.

Outside, George looked around. "I'll bet Bud went to the river."

"He'll be okay, won't he?" Colin couldn't keep the alarm out of his voice.

"Oh, I'm sure he will be. This isn't the first time he's done something goofy, as you might have guessed. It's just that this is probably the messiest."

They walked to the shed, neither one of them speaking much, as Bruno, mindless of the drama at play, chased insects through the grass.

George handed Colin a hammer, and they both began to dismantle the shed.

"I'm really sorry that Bud got you involved in this," George said at last. "It was bad enough that he did what he did to Lolly, but to haul you into it, too, well, that was really too much. Mail-order groom, indeed."

Colin smacked the plank over the window and then pried

the nails out carefully before dropping them in the can that George had for that purpose. "I've been called worse," he said at last.

George swung his head slowly from side to side. "Maybe. But how on earth he came up with that story about you being a mail-order groom is beyond me."

"What, you don't think somebody would send away for me?" Colin grinned.

They laughed.

"I'm a bit concerned that the notebook is missing. Are you sure you moved it to her room?" Colin asked as he carefully removed a bent nail from the window frame.

"I'm sure of it. I put it on the chair in Lolly's room. I figured enough of this tomfoolery had gone on, so let's just get this thing out of circulation."

"Smart. Well, she's sure to find it soon." Colin wiped sweat off his forehead. "I can't believe it's so hot this early. Doesn't bode well for the afternoon."

"We'll probably be baked alive. Since the shed is in the sunlight, let's work on this until noon, and then we can find something else to do in the afternoon."

"Do you ever think about just sitting under a tree and, oh, reading some afternoon?" Colin asked. "I don't think I've ever seen you when you're not doing something here."

"Time is all I've got," George replied somewhat cryptically.

Bruno bounded over to them, a treasure of some kind in his jaws that he dropped at George's feet.

The black-and-white furry creature lifted its tail, identified itself, and ran back into the underbrush.

"It isn't! Please tell me it isn't what I think it is?" Colin drew back as the smell hit him.

"I'm sorry, but it is." George clapped his handkerchief over his nose. "I don't think either of us got that stink on us, do you?"

"I can't tell," Colin said. The smell seemed to permeate everything.

"Hold onto Bruno," George said. "I'll be right back."

The smell was overpowering, and Bruno put his head down and wiped his snout across the scrubby grass, making high-pitched moaning sounds as he did.

"I sure don't blame you, dog," Colin said, trying to breathe as shallowly as possible. "That's nasty."

George returned with two large buckets. "I've got the stuff in here to take care of the skunk stink. Take him to the old cattle tank."

The watering tank was empty, except for two grasshoppers and a rather bored-looking toad hiding in the scattering of leaves.

"Come on, boy," George said to the dog. "You know the routine. In."

The dog jumped into the tank, startling the grasshoppers and the toad into activity. He stopped his whimpering and watched them curiously before trying to catch them.

Colin rescued the creatures from Bruno's paws and set them free.

"This isn't the first time this has happened," George said as he emptied the buckets of two large bottles, a box, and a carton of soap. He dumped the first bottle in one bucket and shook in the contents of the box and stirred it with his hand.

Then he swished the bar of soap through the mixture until it was foamy. He repeated the entire process with the second bucket. "Bruno is a two-bucket dog," he explained. "Now to get this smell out. This ought to do it."

"What goes into it?" Colin asked, leaning over to see.

"It's truly the kitchen sink potion, except that Lolly would never allow me to do this in the kitchen. Heinz white vinegar.

Arm & Hammer baking soda. And good old Fels-Naptha soap."

"And it works?" Colin watched as Bruno sat in the tank, letting George wash him.

"Sure. The key," George said, as he scrubbed the dog with the concoction, "is to get to him right away, before the stink has a chance to set. Skunk'll do that. If you don't clean him up then and there. . ." George shook his head sadly at the thought.

"Why do you do it in the tank? Why not just on the ground?" Colin asked. This was fascinating.

"Because there's a water connection here, and it usually works. It lets me rinse him—" George lifted his hand to point to the pipe, and Bruno seized the chance.

With one leap, he slid free—his fur slicked with the soap— and ran away. Colin started to chase after him, but George called him back. "He's just going to the river. He'll swim in it for a while to get the soap out." He chuckled. "Can't say that he'll smell much better, though. The river is a bit heady this time of year. And speaking of heady, we'd better lather up, too, or Lolly'll have us eating by the barn for the next week or two."

The two of them used the rest of the compound and washed themselves off, even sudsing up their shirts and dungarees.

"Better?" Colin asked, taking a whiff of his shirtsleeve. He couldn't tell if the odor was gone or not.

"Just in case, I think we'd better head down to the river and wash off. Lolly won't want us in the house reeking like this. Of course, after being in the river we won't smell like roses, but it's better than this."

Plus they'd be able to check on Bud, Colin thought.

Lolly was coming out of the house as they walked past, a load of laundry in her hands. "Where are you fellows going?"

"The river," George called back.

"Did you get Bruno cleaned up?" she asked. "You know, I spend more on vinegar and soda and Fels-Naptha on that dog than I do on the rest of us. You're going down to the river to rinse off, I hope, before you bring those clothes back in here. You going to go fishing, too?"

George looked at Colin and for the first time that day, grinned. "What a great idea. Let's grab the poles and see if we can't catch us something."

"You know," Colin said as they got the poles and a pail from the barn, "I'm a bit surprised that we haven't done this before."

George chuckled. "If you'd seen Bud and me try to fish, you'd understand. We're farmers, not fishermen. You asked if I ever take any time off. This is about as close as I get to not doing anything. The fish and I have a deal. I don't bother them and they don't bother me."

"You don't bait your hook?"

"Oh, it's baited but the fish don't care. They either ignore it or eat it right off the hook."

After a quick discussion about what kind of bait was best—George nixed the idea of worms, claiming that dough balls made from bread were just as good since they weren't going to catch anything anyway, so why sacrifice a perfectly good worm's life?—they made a trip into the house to get some bread. Lolly gave them the heel of the loaf from the day before, explaining she had a fresh loaf in the oven, and the two men headed down to the river.

Bud was indeed at the riverside. He'd been in the water already, swimming and working off a head of steam apparently, for he was now sprawled at the shoreline, his shirt and pants still a bit damp. Bruno was splashing happily in the river.

Bud scrambled to his feet when he saw them. "The dog

found himself a skunk, huh? When I saw him tearing through the trees, lathered up like that, I figured he'd either finally gone entirely mad or met himself a skunk."

George looked at him steadily before speaking. "You ran away from us."

Bud shook his head and studied his bare toes that dug into the wet ground at the edge of the river. "I ran away from myself."

"Did it work?" George asked him.

Colin began to step back from them, to move out of this very personal conversation, but George touched his arm. "Stay. You have a stake in this, too."

"No," Bud said. "No matter where I went, I was there. I wasn't getting away from anything. Not that I went anywhere anyway. Just here. But I thought about going somewhere, like Colin did. But I'd still be with me. So I decided to stay. I mean, I was here anyway."

George nodded seriously, but Colin thought he saw a twinkle in the older brother's eyes. "I can't believe it, but I think that made sense in a Bud sort of way."

"Yup," Bud said. "I swam for a while, prayed a little bit, and then I sort of drowsed off."

"Well, we came here to go fishing," Colin said.

"Did you bring me a pole, too?" Bud asked.

George tossed him one, and soon the three of them were sitting on the ramshackle pier, lines in the water. Overhead in the trees, a cluster of birds chatted with each other, and the leaves rustled in the faint breeze against a cloudless sky.

The river made little splashing noises when it spilled onto the shore, and Bruno crashed through the underbrush in search of something interesting.

Sometimes, Colin thought, there was nothing as companionable as silence. It was when people chose not to speak that was telling. He'd known men who would have been unable to tolerate this stillness, who would have found it necessary to fill it up with words.

But silence wasn't a void, not always, and definitely not now. Bud and George's acceptance—and apparent appreciation—of the hush identified them as two who were in touch with their environment and who were able to find harmony in nature.

It was, Colin knew, a rare gift.

Nobody spoke of the thing that Bud had done. Perhaps this was the best way to manage it, Colin thought. Repent in silence, and forgive in silence. Bud certainly seemed a bit more sedate in his behavior. Perhaps he had learned something.

"I should fix this pier," George said, "but for as little as we use it, it seems like such a waste of time."

"It's beautiful down here," Colin said, "so peaceful."

Lolly scrambled down the incline to the shore and stopped suddenly. "Oh, you're all here." She had a fishing pole in her hand, and she stood stock-still, her eyes locked on Bud. "I didn't know—"

The moment hung awkwardly, the pain the family felt spread open and revealed in front of Colin.

Without saying more, she sat beside Colin. She pinched her nose as Bruno joyfully came over to see her, and snuffled around her. "Oh, I can still smell skunk on you! Get away from me."

"Here, boy." George threw a stick into the river and Bruno raced after it. "Sorry, Lolly. I'll keep him out of the house until he's not so awful-smelling."

"You do that. That mongrel's never going to learn about skunks, I'm afraid."

"He had this one in his mouth, and he brought it over to us," Colin explained.

"Wonderful. I gather it was still alive?"

"Quite."

He watched as she rolled a piece of bread into a ball and stuck it on her hook.

"You fish, too?" he asked.

"She's the best of all of us," Bud declared, and Colin breathed easier as she smiled at her brother. Forgiveness came easily to this family, but then, he thought, with a brother like Bud, she probably got a lot of practice.

Bruno came out of the water and settled in the shade— upwind, Colin noted with some amusement.

There was something about fishing that brought people together, he thought. They sat, quietly, letting their hooks sit in the water until whatever bait was on it had surely gone, but not caring. It was being together that mattered.

"Lolly, I'm sorry. I really am," Bud said at last in a low voice. "I act without thinking a lot, and I say things without thinking, too. Actually sometimes I think that I don't think much."

They laughed.

"Bud, I do wish that you wouldn't be so impetuous, but that's part of what makes you who you are," she said. "Someday, I think you'll find a way to harness all that energy you have, and it'll be wonderful; but right now, there are days when I could throttle you."

"There are days when I could throttle myself," Bud said.

This was the right place for him to be, Colin thought as his line floated in the water—at this very moment, in this very spot, with these very people. God was good.

He knew he should think about returning to New York City, to take his place back in the world of commerce; but now, sitting on a pier, dangling a line in the Minnesota River on a late summer afternoon seemed much more important.

The broken links in his memory were almost all mended now, and the spiritual quest that had sent him on his way was nearly complete.

Yet he couldn't bear to leave. Not yet. Maybe not ever.

"This is one of the grand days of summer," Lolly said. "I can feel it in the air off the water. It's like the river is telling us to enjoy this, to store up this warmth, because it's getting to the end. Too soon it'll be September."

September! How long had he been there?

As if reading his mind, she mused, "And to think that it's been just three months, hasn't it, since Colin arrived at our doorstep."

Bud snorted. "Arrived at our fence post, you mean."

Colin shifted uneasily. This conversation had to happen eventually, but he was not looking forward to it at all. He led into it as obliquely as he could. Maybe that would make it easier, although he doubted it.

He took a piece of bread and kneaded it into a ball to be used for bait. He dropped it into the pail and began another one. That one joined the first, and then another and another, and soon the small pail began to fill up.

This was not something he wanted to discuss, but this was as good a time as any, with all of them sitting in the sunlight on the river, fishing poles in their hands.

"You three saved my life."

Bruno left his spot in the shade and trotted over and plopped at his side, dropping a soggy offering of some kind of lake weed at Colin's feet. The smell of the skunk was dissipating a bit, so maybe the dog hadn't received a direct hit after all. Colin reached over and patted the dog's side. "Sorry. You four. Without you, I'd have probably died back there on the road behind your farm."

"It was an honor," George said.

"An honor?" Colin stopped rubbing Bruno's stomach and faced George. "Hardly! I've been a dreadful inconvenience. We all know that these times are making everyone's pocketbook thinner by the day, and yet you took me in, and if you've complained, you haven't done it where I've heard you."

Lolly jiggled her fishing line in the sunlit water. "There's no point in complaining. We don't much believe in it."

Bud snorted. "Remember that the next time you whine about my leaving my socks on the kitchen floor."

"Well, socks on the kitchen floor would make anyone complain. That's unsanitary," Lolly responded.

"Like someone's going to eat off the floor. Even Bruno doesn't do that, do you, big boy?" Bud nudged the dog, who opened one eye slightly before going back to sleep.

"Bruno would eat anything, anywhere, and you know it," George interjected. "The only thing the mutt won't eat is rocks, and even that's just a matter of time. He chewed the handle right off my toolbox last week. And today I had to pull one of your socks out of his mouth. I don't know where he found it."

"On the kitchen floor! I told you. It's disgusting. They smell, for one thing; and for another thing, if you don't pick them up, I have to. And that's nasty. I have to touch your stinky socks with the hands I use to make our dinner, and—"

"Enough!" George thundered. Bruno scrambled to his feet, nearly knocking over the makeshift bait can, and barked. "Bud, just put your socks in the laundry like any other human being. Lolly isn't your servant. And Lolly, don't pick them up any more. Just leave them there until he takes care of them."

"But he won't. And I need to be in the kitchen to cook."

"Then kick them out of the way. . ."

Colin let the argument flow around him like the waters of the river. He knew that they weren't really angry. In fact, it was satisfying, being in a family—

He broke off the thought before it could go any further. This wasn't his family, not really.

He wanted them to be.

The idea struck him with the force of a locomotive. He wanted to be part of this family.

He looked at them, one by one.

Bud's energy. George's stalwartness. Lolly's—Lolly's loveliness.

She was beautiful, but not in a big city sort of way. She wasn't the kind to go smearing on makeup or dolling up her hair with fake waves or color. What she had came from within.

Was it the result of her unshakable faith? Was it the magic that made her eyes sparkle, far beyond what any cosmetic could supply?

And that was one of the reasons he didn't want to leave Valley Junction. He'd wanted to make his life matter, to have meaning, and now, as he watched the sunlight play across Lolly's hair like dappled gold, he wondered how much further he'd have to go.

Maybe he'd already found it, and he was so jaded he didn't really see it?

"Pull it in! Pull it in! You've got something! Oh, for crying out loud, let me have it!" Bud reached across him and snatched the fishing pole and began reeling like mad. "Oh, this has got to be a big one. It's really fighting."

"A big boot, probably." Colin stood and cheered as Bud fought with whatever was on the other end.

Bud's face grew red with the effort, as he walked backward, trying to work the line, until the pole dipped almost to the water's surface. Suddenly it sprang back, nearly knocking Bud into a startled Bruno, who barked furiously at the empty fishing line and the water.

"Well, that was fun," Bud said as he got back to his feet.

"Fun to watch, too," George said. "If I were a wagering man, I'd say that you were snared on a log in there. The lower the water gets, the more debris we'll be catching."

"We won't think about that," Colin declared. "For the record, that was the biggest fish ever caught in Minnesota, and it merely broke free at the last moment."

"A log fish," Lolly said.

He grinned at her. "I never said what kind of record it was, did I?"

Bruno spied something in the river. His nose quivered, his front paw lifted, and his tail raised like a flag. For a moment he was motionless, and then he shot off, splashing into the water and flailing and spattering until Colin tensed, getting ready to go in after him.

Suddenly the dog emerged and trotted victoriously over to George. A catfish almost as long as he was flapped wildly in his jaws and then fell silent.

"Crazy dog caught a fish!" Bud said. "We can't catch anything with fishing lines and hooks and baits, and this mutt dives in and catches a giant fish with his teeth. Where's the fairness in that?"

"Come on," George said, taking the fish from the dog. "This was your fish, Bud. It's still got the hook in its mouth. Bruno just brought it in for you. I guess we're having catfish for dinner. Lolly, we'll see you and Colin later."

"Who's going to clean this stupid fish? I'm not going to," Bud began as they headed toward the house. "How come I always have to do the dirty jobs around here? Why don't Lolly and Colin have to—"

His voice faded away as they walked through the trees lining the river.

"There's that complaining thing again," Lolly said. "That

boy's mouth goes all the time."

"He's a good kid. Energetic." He picked up the fishing pole with the broken line and rewound it.

Lolly laughed. "Definitely energetic. I wish I had even a particle of his liveliness. I feel like a slug around him sometimes."

"I feel like a slug today, that's for sure. Hey, Lolly. Look over there, toward the west. Doesn't it look like there might be some weather coming our way?"

"Could be. Oh, some rain would be so nice. Maybe this heat would break then."

"Well, until then, I'm going into the water." He slid off the pier and, bending his knees, let himself sink up to his chin. George was right. The river was quite shallow there. Now that he wasn't on the platform any more, he could see the watermarks on pilings. They were mute testimony to the falling levels.

He pulled himself back out and sprawled on the pier, letting the sun dry his clothes on him. "I could stay here forever."

"Then do."

He struggled upright. "Lolly, as much as I want to, I can't."

She turned her head, but not before he saw the flicker of pain that twisted her face. "Then don't."

"I don't want to keep taking advantage of you." He sought the words that simply would not come, and he shrugged helplessly.

"You're not taking advantage of us," she said, her words tight in the summer afternoon. "You work."

"Not well." He tried a laugh but it faded on his lips. "I'm not a farmer, Lolly. I'm a businessman."

"Well, that explains it. You can't be a farmer and a business-man? I suppose not, not in these times." She still wouldn't look at him.

He took her hands. They were rough, the fingernails split. A scratch ran across the back of one of them, and he ran his thumb down the raised red welt. "Lolly, I want to stay. I do. I don't want to leave you."

She turned at last. Her eyes brimmed with tears. "But you're going to, aren't you?"

The world spun crazily. He couldn't.

He had her in his arms, and her face was in his shoulder, and his hand was in her hair, and then his lips were on her cheek, and on her mouth, and she was kissing him back, and everything changed.

He couldn't live without her. He just couldn't.

&

Lolly paused, trying to identify the sound. Bruno was outside barking at something, a series of sharp excited yips—so whatever she heard, he did, too.

Ping. Ping. Pingpingping. Ping. Ping.

It couldn't be. Could it?

She wiped her hands on her apron and ran out the door. Her brothers and Colin met her by the coop.

"It's raining!"

"It really is!"

The four of them stood in the yard, their faces up to heaven, and let the droplets fall on their faces.

"Thank You, God!" she called out. "Thank You!"

Rain! Had anything ever felt as good?

She smiled as the drops soaked her. Yes, something had.

Colin had kissed her.

eight

The last days of summer are filled with promises—promises given and promises kept. These days are precious, the final hurrah of the sun's bright fire. He takes me in his arms, and he vows the great promises of summer. We speak of stories that will keep us warm through winter's cold blast, of kisses that can catch snowflakes, of love that knows no end. He promises he will stay. . .

Bliss. That was what this was all about, Lolly thought. Just bliss. The chickens clucked happily as Colin spread corn for them. He'd learned quite a bit since his arrival there. She smiled as she remembered the first time he'd fed the chickens. He'd dropped the feed in a circle around him and found himself surrounded by a tight ring of hungry poultry that would not move for anything.

He'd had to stand there, motionless, until they'd finished their meal.

But now he knew how to do it so he wasn't hemmed in. Maybe he could be both a businessman and a farmer.

She scolded herself at the thought. *One kiss, and you've got yourself married off. Hold on, Lolly! He isn't your mail-order groom!*

Still, it was nice to dream. Now that the joy of the notebook was taken away—she didn't even know where it had gone—she'd had to keep her story going in her head. It had taken a very interesting turn recently, too, she thought.

She smiled at the dish towel with the happy teakettle

embroidered on it. She smiled at the hairbrush. She smiled at the petunias, now perky after the rain.

She smiled through church, even beaming at Hildegard Hopper and Amelia Kramer, who looked at her with ill-disguised interest. Reverend Wellman's sermon, about the meaning of grace, seemed absolutely on track, and Lolly's heart swelled with love for all her fellow human beings. The hymns were all familiar ones, and she sang with enthusiasm.

After the service had ended, Hildegard and Amelia made a beeline for her, exclaiming over the rain and how it must have truly benefited Lolly's petunias.

"So," Hildegard said, the magenta flower on her hat quivering as she took one of Lolly's elbows and Amelia, in her usual navy blue dress, took the other, "are we having a nice dinner today?"

"We?" Lolly didn't remember inviting them, but she felt so good that she was ready to serve soup and sandwiches to the entire world. "Of course, you're invi—"

George swooped in, leaving Ruth standing in front of the church with an amused expression on her face, and rescued Lolly from the two women. "Dear sister, I'm so sorry to interrupt this conversation, but we really must go. Bud needs to get home. The chickens, you know."

The two women recoiled in horror at the mention of the chickens. Bud shook his head and pointed out loudly that Colin had already fed them, but George was insistent and hustled them all into the truck. Bruno, who'd been sleeping under the truck, jumped in the back.

"Why did you do that?" she asked, so squished into the seat that she could feel Bud's ribs on one side and George's belt on the other. There really wasn't room for all four of them in the cab. "We were chatting so nicely and—"

"There's no such thing as a nice chat with those two,"

George said, frowning at the road. "Plus you were just on the verge of asking them to come to dinner."

Pandemonium broke out in the truck as Bud began railing about Hildegard and Amelia, Colin tried to calm him down, George started yelling at Lolly about her lapse in good judgment, and Lolly hollered back at him. Bruno howled over the entire thing.

At last they pulled up in front of the farm. As they spilled out, Bud said grumpily, "It's a good thing we're too poor to be fat, or we'd never fit in there."

"Finally," Lolly said, grinning again. "Something positive to say about being broke!"

After their dinner, Colin helped Lolly clear the table. "I'll dry," he offered as she filled the sink with dishes.

She felt that all-over smile coming on again. He needed a haircut. His dark brown hair was spilling over his shirt collar at the nape of his neck, and he had a little puff of soapsuds on one cheek. She'd never seen anyone as handsome as he was. Mail-order groom? Sure! She'd have picked him immediately from the catalog—if that was indeed how someone would get a mail-order groom.

George stood at the door. His face was solemn. "Can you two come into the living room, please?"

"You sound so serious," she said. "Just let me finish—"

"Now."

She'd never seen him look so grave, nor heard him speak so abruptly.

"Colin, come on." She took her apron off and hung it over the back of the chair.

Bud was already in the living room, and from the baffled expression on his face, she could tell he didn't know what this was about either.

George pulled his chair closer to the little table. In his

hand was a ledger. Lolly recognized it. It was the same one that their parents had used. They'd just started it when they'd died, and George had used it ever since.

He opened the ledger and sighed.

"I hate to say this. I've gone over the numbers again and again. I was up all night praying, trying to decide if this was the right thing to do."

As he paused, Lolly studied her brother's face. Dark circles rimmed his eyes, and lines were etched deeply between his eyebrows into a constant frown. He looked exhausted.

Colin moved closer to her, as if offering her support.

"Go on," she said to her brother.

"The wheat isn't going to come in at all where I'd hoped it would. There just wasn't enough moisture this year. We'll be lucky if we break even."

"But the harvest isn't in," Colin said. "Maybe it could rebound."

George shook his head. "The kernels are shriveled. You can walk through the fields and hear it, that rattling sound. The stalks are like the skeletons of the wheat. We can't do it. I can't keep the farm together any longer."

"What are you saying?" she asked, unable to take in what her ears were hearing.

"I'm saying that we're going to have to sell it." His shoulders slumped. "That is, assuming we can even find a buyer."

"But I don't understand," Bud said. "I thought we owned the farm, that it was paid for."

"It is," George answered. "But we're in debt for the other things. We haven't made a profit in a couple of years. Honestly, I don't think anyone has."

Lolly put her face in her hands. This was horrible, beyond understanding. How could this have happened?

Colin put his hand on her back and murmured something

reassuringly. "There's no other way?" he asked George.

George pushed the ledger to him. "You're a businessman. Take a look and see if you can see an escape route. I sure can't."

Bud looked at Lolly, and in his eyes she knew was reflected her own fear. "Colin will find something. Just watch, he will."

She knew what the answer was going to be—it would be the same for them as it was for thousands of others. They were going to lose their home.

Everything that their parents had sacrificed for, everything the three children had worked for with the goal of keeping the farm as their home—it was all going to be lost to creditors.

It was an entirely too-familiar saga.

She stood up and walked back to the kitchen. There were dishes to be washed.

Dishes that would be sold and put into cupboards that would belong to someone else. Spoons and forks and knives laid into drawers that would be used by another set of hands.

It all seemed unreal, like a dream that she would wake up from at any moment and wonder about. Like a replay of that horrible day five years ago, when George had told them that their parents had died. Time ceased making sense as her mind tried to sort through this life-changing news.

A horn outside announced visitors.

"Get rid of them," Bud said to her from the doorway of the kitchen. "This isn't the time for guests."

Her mind wouldn't form a coherent thought. All she could think of was that she was losing the farm.

She pasted on a smile and went outside. The two women had the doors to the DeSoto open, and Hildegard was heaving herself out with effort as Amelia delicately swung her legs onto the ground.

Hildegard immediately began fanning her face with her

hand. "Whew! It's muggy down here by the river." Beads of sweat populated her forehead and cheeks. "I'd have thought the rain would have taken care of that, but it's still so close."

"I don't think it's this bad in town," Amelia contributed, her face screwed into a dainty frown. "It's probably all these trees and plants and such."

Lolly held up her hand. "I'm sorry, but this isn't a good time for a visit."

Hildegard's gloved hand flew to her rather substantial chest and with a great show of concern, she asked, "Is everyone all right? No one is sick, I hope! Oh, my goodness!"

The woman was a terrible actress, Lolly thought. Her false sincerity would fool no one.

"One person falls ill, and the next thing you know, everyone in town is sick, too," Amelia said. "That's the way plagues start."

Hildegard nodded so vehemently that the feather in her hat bobbed crazily. "The plague. Like the flu epidemic in '18. Of course, you're too young to remember that, Lolly."

"No, Hildegard, dear, she wouldn't even have been born then," Amelia said.

"I was born in 1916," Lolly said, wondering why she was even part of this absurd conversation. What did it matter how old she was during the flu epidemic?

"Nevertheless, we learned then, didn't we? One cough in church. That's all it takes." Amelia fairly quivered with self-righteousness.

"Who coughed in church?" Hildegard looked alarmed.

"No one coughed in church," Lolly said, but the older woman was not going to be swayed from the idea.

"Was it Bud? George? Colin?" Hildegard leaned forward eagerly. "Is Colin the one who's ill? Oh, poor thing! I'd better see to him right now."

She began to bustle toward the door, despite Lolly's protestations. "No one is sick! That's not it at all! Please, stop! No one is ill!"

"But you said that Colin had the flu," Amelia said, her lips pursing in disapproval. "And on a Sunday, too. Not nice to lie on a Sunday." She shook a gloved finger in Lolly's face.

"I didn't—" Lolly began, but a great ruckus from the back interrupted her.

"Lolly! The chickens!"

Colin tore around the house, a frantic chicken in his grasp. Its wings flapped wildly, and feathers floated around him.

The two women retreated immediately to the DeSoto, and as Hildegard pulled out of the driveway, she called out, "Colin, you shouldn't be out, not as sick as you are! Fluids, that's the answer. Fluids and sleep."

The chicken calmed down as soon as the automobile cruised out of sight behind the bend in the road, and Colin put it back on the ground. It immediately picked its way back to the yard behind the house.

"What was that all about?" She pointed at the chicken, which paused to shake its feathers into place.

"I thought you could use some help, so I intervened with the chicken."

"What was wrong with it? It sure was upset."

He grinned. "I was hugging it. Chickens don't like to be hugged."

"Ah." She stood still, unsure what to do next.

"They don't like to be hugged, but I do," he said, and he opened his arms.

She stood in his embrace, drawing strength from him. She could feel his heart beating, the rhythm regular and strong. With each breath his chest rose and fell, while his fingers wrapped themselves in her hair, and the bun loosened, the ribbon sliding off, and she didn't care.

When she was in his arms, there were no money worries. The farm was safe. Her future was secured. If only she could stay there forever.

If only.

She could hear her brothers in the background, and she didn't care. This moment was hers and Colin's.

He kissed the top of her head and hugged her tightly. "You're so much nicer than a chicken to hug."

"You say the sweetest things," she answered.

"They call me sugar mouth," he murmured.

"They do?" She felt the smile begin again as she lifted her head for what she knew was coming.

Kissing. What a wonderful thing it was, she thought as their lips met. She understood now why it was so valued— and why it was so dangerous.

She didn't want for it to end, but something sharp jabbed into her foot, and she screamed against his mouth.

"I'm sorry!" he said, pulling away immediately, but she shook her head and looked down.

Around them were many of the chickens, pecking at their feet. She soon realized why.

"Colin, I hate to say this, but I believe we're standing on an anthill."

As if to prove the truth of her words, two chickens picked off more of the little black insects from her feet, and the rooster, Floyd, strutted over to see what the buffet was all about. He started in on Colin's feet, his beak tapping rapidly on Colin's shoes.

"You know," he said with a laugh as he shooed the birds and they scattered, "I thought your brothers would be our chaperones, but they're ignoring us. The chickens, though—do you suppose they don't want us kissing?"

"They'd better watch it or they'll end up as fried chicken," she said, reluctant to leave the harbor of his arms.

A stray breeze picked up a strand of her hair and ruffled it. He smoothed it back into place and kissed her forehead. "You're tough. But I like that. We need to—"

"Colin and Lolly are kissing, Colin and Lolly are kissing!" Bud sang from behind the chicken coop. Bruno dashed out and ran in circles around them, barking happily.

"Stop it, Bud," she said. "That's terribly rude. And childish. And stupid. And hush up, Bruno. Just because you're with Bud doesn't mean you have to act like him."

"George wants you to quit smooching and come inside," her brother said, ignoring her little tirade. "He wants to talk to you some more. Probably about the farm."

❧

George was standing at the window, looking out over the farm. "Even if Colin can find some little bit of something I've overlooked—and I don't see how, not as often as I've gone over the accounts—we're going to have to figure out what to do. First off, like I said, selling the farm is going to have to happen."

"How much do we owe?" Lolly asked.

Her older brother shook his head. "It's not that. We really don't owe anything except taxes and a small bill at the store in town."

"Then we could cut back," Bud said.

George sighed and rubbed his forehead. "We've cut our electricity use to almost nothing. Our food is pretty much what we get from the garden here, and what we don't grow, Lolly gets through trade with the store for the eggs."

"So what's the problem?" Bud asked. "If we're okay, why can't we just stay on the farm?"

"There's more than that. There's gasoline for the truck—it's not much, but it still has to be paid. Things break and have to be replaced. And let's not forget that winter is coming, and this farm's income comes to a complete halt then. How can we heat this place? And food? Lolly can put some aside with canning and such, but nowhere near enough to get us through a Minnesota winter. Even if I cut down every single tree on the property, it won't keep us warm until next summer."

She had never heard George say so much at one time.

"There are programs," Colin said, "new things the government is trying. Like the Works Project. Have you looked into that?"

"I sure don't want to have to rely on the government," George said, clearly uncomfortable with the idea that he hadn't been able to provide himself.

"I think they're doing something in Mankato," Lolly said, "but that's probably too far away. There's no way to live here in Valley Junction and work in Mankato. And in the winter—" She shuddered. "That would be a terrible drive to have to make every day."

"The bad state the economy is in has got to end, I'm sure of that," George said. "I'd hoped we could wait it out by being prudent with what we had, but we ran out of steam before it did."

"The drought hasn't helped a thing, either." Lolly thought of the carrots that she'd dug up last night. The downpour hadn't done much to help the shriveled roots that looked more like tiny gnarled orange fingers than like the plump carrots they should have been.

"But it's got to break. I really think that it'll end soon." Colin's voice rang out confidently in the small room. "God won't let this go on forever."

Bud shook his head. "I don't know. I know it's not true, but doesn't it sometimes seem like God has forgotten us? That maybe there's a little stretch of the U.S.A. that He's missed? A place called Minnesota?"

"It's everywhere," George said gloomily. "Not just here."

She'd never heard them talk like this before, and her soul stung with their pain.

It did seem like they'd been forgotten, but she'd never gotten to the stage they were at, where they were actually doubting God.

"God is with us," she said gently. "He is. He was with us before, through those terrible days five years ago, when we thought the world was over."

"We were right, apparently," Bud muttered.

"You don't really believe that, do you?" she asked him, covering his hand with hers. She knew he didn't think it was true. This was just Bud's way, to blurt out whatever crossed his mind.

"Nah, I guess not," he admitted. "But you've got to admit that God sure does like to test us a lot. And I don't know why."

"That's what faith is all about," Lolly said. "It's being sure that even if we don't understand why things are happening the way they do, that we know there's a purpose, a goal. God understands suffering. We just have to trust that this is going to work out. We need faith."

"Oh, I guess I've got faith, all right," Bud said. "I do know that there's more to our lives than this particular moment, and in twenty or forty or fifty years, I'll probably look back on this and say, 'My, but didn't we have fun.' Still, I'll tell you what, if God would like to put a gold mine in our backyard today, I'd be fine with that!"

They all laughed at Bud's honesty.

"I suppose there's always the chance that could happen," Colin said, "but I kind of think we shouldn't wait for it. Barring a gold mine under the chicken coop, the government

will help out more. It has to. There's too much at stake."
Bruno sat up, his tail thumping in anticipation. "S-t-a-k-e,
you goofy dog, not s-t-e-a-k."

"Like we've seen s-t-e-a-k around here lately," Bud said
morosely.

"The time will come when you will eat steak, and maybe
you won't have diamond-encrusted belts and shirts made of
silk, but you'll be fine. I just know you will."

George sighed. "I'm glad you can be that certain, and while
I do trust the Lord, I'm still going to want to see a real dollar
now and then."

Lolly's stomach twisted. This wasn't just a theoretical discussion about the effects of this economic depression. This
was real life, *her* life.

They were going to lose the farm, the place that had been
their home for their entire lives, the fields that their parents
had nurtured and cared for, the house that her father—and
mother—had built with their own hands, knowing that a
family not only needed each other but something to call their
own. They'd chosen land.

"Mom and Dad bought this land and built the old house
and then this house themselves," she said softly. "Mom had
been saving her sewing money in a baking soda box in her
stockings drawer. Remember how she told the story? Then
one day she didn't get the drawer all the way shut, and their
cat pulled the drawer out, found the box and chewed on it.
She laughed and said that was one time when she was lucky
that she didn't get paid in paper money. The cat couldn't hurt
the coins, just the box."

George picked up the story. "Dad had tucked away his
'summer money'—the extra that he got from clearing out the
gophers on the neighbor's farm. After they knew they were
going to get married, they each lived at home and worked,

Mom as a teacher and Dad as a clerk at a grocery store, and they saved every penny. They had already chosen this piece of land and drawn up the plans for the house, down to what doorknobs they wanted. That's what they saved for."

"Mom told me that they added that to the money they got from their wedding. They were counting every penny." Bud chuckled. "She said she was horribly disappointed when the banker and his wife gave them the crystal vase. They were so focused on saving money for a home that she didn't realize how expensive that vase was."

"That's the vase," Lolly said, pointing it out on the corner shelf. "How it's made it through three children and a rambunctious dog or two without even a chip in it is amazing."

"This is the only way we were allowed to look at it." Bud stood up and walked over to the shelf. He put his hands behind his back and laced his fingers together, and Lolly laughed at the memory.

"Our hands had to be locked together behind us," she said. "That way, she told us, they couldn't get in trouble. She used to say, 'One hand watches the other,' which made Dad laugh every time. It wasn't until I got older that I realized she was making a play on words for 'One hand washes the other.'"

"I still don't get it," Bud said as he walked back to his chair.

Colin grinned at Lolly as her brother continued, "Well, do you? One hand does wash the other." He shrugged his shoulders in defeat. "So why do people keep saying it?"

"It means that if you do something nice for me, I will probably do something nice for you," George said. "It's not about washing your hands."

"Then why—oh, never mind." Bud reached down and took a soggy piece of brown cloth out of Bruno's mouth. "Does anyone know what this used to be?"

"I'm pretty sure it's my work glove," Colin said, waving

away the wet scrap of fabric that Bud offered him. "No thanks. Bruno can have it. It doesn't seem to have all the fingers on it anymore, so I can't think it's worth saving."

Lolly stood up and directed Bruno to the door. "Out. Now."

"Come on, Lolly," Bud said. "He wasn't doing anything."

"Right. Not much. Just drooling on the floor and leaving shreds of Colin's glove under the table." She scowled at her brother.

"So?"

"So do you think he's going to pick the pieces up?"

"Just leave them there. He'll eat them sooner or later," Bud answered cheerfully. "Or you can grind them up and use them in our meat loaf."

Meat loaf. The world was falling apart and her brother was talking about work gloves and meat loaf!

&

Colin walked down to the river. The recent rain seemed to have revitalized the mosquitoes, and he swatted them away impatiently.

George's news put an entirely different face on his situation. The mail-order groom fiasco was reduced to just that—a fiasco. They could live through that. This was more important.

A sense of urgency pounded through him, even if the Prescott family seemed to be resigned to the loss. There had to be some way to save this farm. There was a family heritage on the line. He couldn't let it go without doing something.

The family needed some way of sustaining itself until the economy righted itself. It might be a year. It might be ten.

What could he do to help them? He had money back in New York. Or at least he might have. When he'd left in June, he hadn't exactly taken care of all the loose ends that would result from his sudden departure. No, he'd just assumed someone would clean up after him. He shook his head as he thought back to the life he had led.

But the point was that he had been financially secure. He had money. The problem was how to get it to them. He knew they wouldn't accept it from him, even as a loan, and certainly not as a gift.

No, it had to be more than that.

He sat on the pier, and immediately the swarm of mosquitoes surrounded his head and arms. God must have had something in mind for them, but right now Colin couldn't see the purpose. They were like the depression and the drought. Somehow they fit into God's grand plan, but just how, he couldn't see.

One thing was becoming very clear. He couldn't stay here. Every bit of food he ate and every drop of water he used in washing hastened the demise of their home. He had to leave, and quickly.

Unless he could help them.

He weighed his options, such as they were, and only one option seemed possible.

If he was going to find a way to help them, he couldn't do it here. Perhaps if he went back to New York, he might be able to think of something.

Plus there was the very real fact that his separation from Lolly might make him work even that much harder to resolve the problem.

The mosquitoes were relentless. They bit through his clothes, attacked his eyelids, and crawled along his ears.

"This might help," Lolly said as she sat down beside him. "It's a mixture I make up, but mainly it's just citronella oil. We use it when the mosquitoes are bad, like they are now."

She opened a small bottle and poured some out in her hand. With practiced moves, she wiped it over his face and the back of his neck, and then his hands. "Run your hands over your trousers and ankles, too," she advised.

Almost instantly the pesky insects dispersed. "Thanks," he said, as she recapped the bottle and put it back into her pocket. "They were about to send me back to the house. I don't think I could have borne being out here with them much longer."

Lolly's legs dangled over the edge of the pier, and she swung them back and forth. "They can be insistent, that's for sure."

"That's true."

The sun was high in the sky, baking off the last remnants of the rain from the day before. Only along the water's edge, where the sun hadn't penetrated entirely through the woods, had he been able to smell the humid reminder of the shower.

"It's very pretty here," he said, watching the river's surface reflect the bright daylight in a mottled display of gold and bronze and taupe.

"I love September trees, but they're a bit sad, you know."

"September trees are sad?" He glanced at her, but she was smiling faintly at the opposite shoreline.

"Of course. This is the end of summer, the last stretch of time when they know they'll have their leaves. Come October, the leaves will begin to fall, not a lot at first, but it'll start." She stopped suddenly, and he thought he knew why.

"Are you thinking about this October?" he asked.

She nodded, and he saw a tear slide down her cheek. "I know what I have to do, except I don't know how to do it. Everything in my life is changing. I don't even know if we'll stay here in Valley Junction."

"Will you all stay together?" he asked, putting his hand over hers.

"I don't know. George is very fond of Ruth, and I'd thought they'd end up getting married eventually—once he knew I was seen to." Her face reddened, and she added very quickly, "But without a home or a job, that won't happen. He wouldn't ask her to live on Relief."

She sniffled, and he handed her his handkerchief. She took it and wiped the tears away, even as new ones were replacing them.

He didn't interrupt as she continued.

"And Bud—I don't know what we'll do about Bud. He's a bit of a loose cannon, if you know what I mean. He's a good kid, but he needs someone with him to keep him contained. So I guess that he'll go with either Bud or me, or both of us."

She shook her head. "We'll all be together still, I guess. I have no skills, and neither does Bud. George can do all sorts of things, but it's a matter of someone hiring him. And what are we supposed to do? Just go on the road, like hoboes?"

She gasped. "Oh, I didn't mean that! Colin, please, please, forgive me!"

He rubbed the back of her hand with his thumb, and looked into her river-dark eyes. "Not a problem."

She still looked so horrified at what she'd said that he laughed. "Lolly, dear, please stop worrying. I wasn't offended by what you said. I know what you meant. Having to sell the farm is traumatic. It's not just a loss of some property. It's a loss of an entire lifestyle." Lolly still appeared so aghast at her words that he did the only thing he could reasonably do. He took her in his arms and kissed her.

Again, and again, and again.

He was never going to leave.

&

They walked back to the house, their fingers intertwined. Although they hadn't spoken of love, Lolly knew that for her, at least, her heart had been given over entirely. She loved him, and yet she was afraid of it.

Yesterday, it had been different. Yesterday, the depression hadn't come up to their door and walked right in. Yesterday, their tomorrows were the next step in the line of years.

They stopped on the edge of the field. The farm was framed in golden sunlight, set against a backdrop of a natural shelterbelt. From here, no one could tell that the world had ground to a sudden and ugly stop at this very spot.

Even love couldn't cushion this blow.

"It's beautiful," he said, his grip tightening on her hand.

"I want to remember it always, just the way it is now," she whispered. "One day I will tell my children about this place, about the love that was built into the floorboards and the walls and the ceilings, and about how a man came here, at the end, and what he brought to my life."

As long as he stood beside her, she was strong.

"You saved my life," he said. "In so many ways, you saved me. My kind-hearted woman."

He let go of her hand and spread his fingers across her cheeks. His thumbs ran over the bones under her eyes, and traced down the side of her face. "Lolly," he said. "Lolly."

She was astonished to see his eyes brimming with unshed tears.

"What's wrong?" she asked, and then she laughed shakily. "Aside from knowing that we're losing our home?"

"How can our lives be so beautiful, and yet so torn apart? How can I choose this day to tell you, when I know that your world has been pulled from under you—"

He paused.

"Tell me what?" she prompted.

"That I love you."

nine

The last days of summer slip through my fingers like kernels of wheat, dried in the sun. So this is the harvest of my love? Lonely days become even lonelier. Once one knows love, a spot becomes created for it in the heart, and whenever love is gone, that place is an aching abyss. My soul aches for him. My heart cries for the love we knew. Where does love go? Does it die, like the last grasses of August?

"I told her that I love her." There. The words were out in the open, ready to take on their own life.

He felt better, knowing that he wasn't keeping a secret from Lolly's brothers. It had kept him sleepless almost every night for the past two weeks, worrying about whether it was right not to let them in on his feelings for their sister.

"No fooling!" Bud clapped Colin on the back.

"What did she say?" George asked, not looking up from the pile of boards from the back barn that he was pulling nails from. Not having been used in several years, it had fallen into disrepair. Now that the utility shed was down, he was attacking the back barn, too. "Bud, you have to be more careful when you put the lumber over here. If you don't take the nails out first, someone, like me, is going to step on one and drive it right through his shoe."

"Sure." Bud pulled another board off the nearly dismantled barn and tossed it toward George.

"Didn't you hear me? Look at this!" George held the offending board in front of him and pointed at a nail sticking

121

out from the side of it. "Take the nail out before you put the board on the pile. Put the nail in the can." He shook the can of nails. "Here. Goes in here."

"Why don't you show me how?" Bud asked with a sideways grin at Colin. "Show me what you mean."

"Yeah, you think I'm going to fall for that?" his brother grumbled as he pulled the nail out and dropped it into the can and then neatly placed the board on the stack.

"You just did." Bud laughed and George rolled his eyes.

He couldn't leave this family, Colin thought. He'd have to think of some way to stay here and help support them, both financially and emotionally. He owed them at least that much.

And the fact was that he was in love with Lolly. It still took him by surprise how quick and effective the process had been. He had, truth be told, lost his heart when he'd opened his eyes and seen her leaning over him, her hair that would not stay put falling around her face, her dark gray eyes searching his face, her fair brow furrowed with concern.

She had, from that day on, moved into his heart, completely and fully. How could he even think about leaving here? About leaving her?

"So what are your intentions toward my sister?" Bud asked as he tugged yet another board free and pitched it, nails still in it, onto the pile that George had just straightened. George rocked back on his heels and glared at Bud.

"What?" Bud asked George innocently.

George didn't answer. Instead he dramatically picked up the board, removed the nails, and one by one, dropped each nail into the can. Then he carefully placed the plank onto the pile and returned to his work.

"Slow learner," Bud said to Colin out of the corner of his mouth.

"Let's do this," Colin offered. "You pull the board out. Hand it to me. I'll take the nails out and put them in the can. I'll give the board to George, and he can put it on the stack."

"Assembly line," George said. "Brilliant. I feel silly that I didn't think of it earlier myself."

"And he calls himself the smart one," Bud said with a wink.

"Did *you* think of it?" George snapped back. "Ah. I thought not."

"See? He thought not. That means he doesn't think."

The back-and-forth between the two brothers lent an air of normalcy to the day, so much so that he was caught off guard when Bud picked up the earlier thread of conversation. "Are you going to tell us what she said when you told her you loved her?"

"A gentleman doesn't kiss and tell," George said almost primly.

"Yeah, but we're talking about Colin now."

"I honestly don't remember what she said," Colin said as he took the next board from Bud. "Maybe nothing."

"You weren't kissing her, were you?" George asked, leaning on the plank that Colin handed him.

"Maybe." Colin wiped his face with his handkerchief. It was one thing to tell George and Bud that he was in love with Lolly. It was another thing entirely to discuss the kiss. That was private and pure. "Here's the deal. I do love Lolly. I know I haven't known her long enough to dare to ask her to marry me, and maybe that's not where this will go, but she is special to me."

"I'm not sure the timing on this is good," George said, his face serious.

"The timing is terrible," Colin admitted. "I had no intention of telling her what my feelings were. The words just took wing and flew right out of my mouth."

"And how did you feel afterwards?" George kept his gaze steadily on Colin's face.

"Like a weight had been lifted off my shoulders. Off my heart. I knew it was the right thing to say."

"I see." Lolly's older brother returned to the lumber stack. "I'd say it's the real thing then."

"Listen to him." Bud joined the discussion. "Mr. Expert-in-Love himself. You learn all this from Ruth?"

His older brother abandoned the woodpile and approached Bud, his eyes blazing with anger. "You leave Ruth out of this."

Colin understood George's fury. The decision to sell the farm had taken his future away from him, and without even the basics of a home and a job, he certainly couldn't pursue the young woman's affections.

"Fine, fine!" Bud lifted his hands in surrender.

George stood still, his face reddened with emotion, until at last he turned, knocking over the can of nails, and stalked away, his hands shoved into his pants pockets.

"What was that all about?" Bud asked, watching his brother leave. "I didn't mean anything by it."

"I'm guessing that he is quite in love with Ruth, and that he's quite committed to her and to being with her." Colin knelt down and began to pick up the scattered nails.

"That's for sure. Have you ever seen him at the café? I practically have to pull him out of there with a towrope to get him to go."

"How does Ruth feel about him?"

"Oh, she's just as goo-goo about him as he is about her."

"They might have been making plans for a life together, or maybe they were just thinking about it, wouldn't you say?"

"Sure."

"I'm wondering," Colin said carefully, "if the prospect of losing the farm has destroyed their dreams."

The fact was that he had studied the ledger George had kept. How Lolly's brother had managed to keep them all on the farm without going into debt was nothing short of a miracle.

But it seemed that the time for miracles on this farm had come to an end. There were precious few pennies on this farm, and he could see no way to squeeze any more out of them than George already had.

He wasn't used to praying, at least not like Reverend Wellman, with *Thou* and *Thee* and *wilt*. The best he could do was tell God what he wanted and leave the rest up to the Divine.

On Sunday, Reverend Wellman had preached about the plow. You could pray for a plow, and maybe a friend lends you one, or a neighbor moves and gives you his. You strike it rich and buy a plow. So you've got a plow.

But that doesn't mean your fields are plowed, and that's what matters.

You've got to put your back into the work, the minister had told them, and do it. That's how God works through you. He gives you the plow—the capability—and it's up to you to use that plow.

Even as he changed the subject to the heat, and as he and Bud exchanged predictions on if and when it might break, a wordless prayer circled through his heart—one that asked for help, for relief, for grace, and for mercy.

And for a solution.

※

Bruno circled her feet, his toenails clicking on the linoleum, as Lolly cut the beans for the hot dish, a mixture of pasta and vegetables and leftover beef. If she diced everything a bit finer, the vegetables didn't look so peaked and the meat went a little further.

"If I carve any more corners off the food," she said aloud to the dog, "there won't be anything left."

For the past hour, she'd heard the men talking outside. They were too far away to make out individual words. Just the ribbon of sound floated to her.

Now they had stopped, and she couldn't hear the sound of the hammer on the wood of the outbuilding they were taking down.

"They probably went swimming," she said as she leaned over and lit the stove. "I don't know why I'm doing this. It's so hot I could put it on the counter and it'd bake up just fine."

Bruno yawned loudly, and she gave him the bone from the roast. "Here you go, you goofy mutt." He snapped it up in his jaws and carried it under the table, where he plopped down and chewed on it.

There wasn't much meat on the bone at all. She'd taken every possible scrap off it already, but she knew the dog would carry the bone around for days, protectively guarding it against any and all threats.

"Don't worry," she said. "I won't fight you for it. And I don't think anyone else will, either."

She tucked her hair back into the bun. One of these days she'd go ahead and bob it, just cut the whole scraggly thing off and be done with it. She looked longingly at the kitchen shears, but satisfied herself with twirling it in a loose knot and retying it.

She walked through the house, straightening a pillow on the couch, wiping down the shelves by the window. She paused at the crystal vase and she carefully took it down and sat with it on the sofa, cradling the precious object in her lap.

With the edge of her apron, she cleaned the dust from the etched surface. She licked the tip of her finger and ran it around the edge, and was rewarded with a shrill sound that brought Bruno running, the bone clenched in his jaws.

"Sorry," she said, laughing as he hid under the table. He stared out at her with suspicious eyes. "Didn't like that, I gather?"

"Didn't like what?" Colin asked as he entered the room and sat beside her. "He doesn't like crystal?"

"I made it sing, like this." She wet her finger and ringed the top of the vase, again producing the piercing note.

"That's singing?" Colin asked, wrinkling his nose. "I'm with you, Bruno. That hurts my ears."

Lolly put the vase back on the table. "Here it is. The best thing we own. I wonder what it would fetch if we sold it."

"Not much, I'm afraid," he said. "You're better off to hold on to it and the memories that go with it. Those are priceless, you know."

"I don't need priceless. I need something with a price."

She didn't mean to sound glum, but it was unavoidable. She'd carried the news of the impending sale with her for over two weeks now. It was like a heavy cloak, settling on her shoulders and weighing her down. Every once in a while she'd forget, but something would remind her and again, she'd feel the pressure.

She stood up and put the vase back on the shelf. "*Pfft*," she said. "After all these years of dusting this vase, I thought I might get something in exchange." She tried for a cheerfulness she didn't feel.

"We'll figure something out," he said from the couch.

"I like that. *We*."

"George is going in to Mankato on Friday, he says. He's going to check into that program the government has now, and he's also going to see if there's any kind of help the family can get in the interim."

"Relief? We're going to have to go on Relief?" Her shoulders sagged in defeat and she leaned against the wall.

George had once characterized Relief as the last door in the hall, the one you thought was an exit but was instead another office. They had vowed never to take advantage of it—but they hadn't envisioned their situation getting so desperate.

"Relief isn't a bad thing," Colin said. "The economy's condition is a bad thing. The drought is a bad thing. But Relief isn't."

"I can't do this. I just can't do this anymore." She buried her face in her hands.

She felt his arms go around her, and she leaned into his welcome strength.

"Don't cry," he whispered as he stroked her hair. "We can make do. Don't cry."

"I'm not crying." Her words were muffled against his shirt collar. She breathed in his scent, a mixture of sun and sweat. "I'm too drained to cry. It seems like everything is make do, make do, make do. I've cut the carrots for dinner so tiny they're nothing more than little orange flakes. The meat in the hot dish is there in name only. Tonight we can play a game called Find the Beef. I used the last of the noodles, and I don't know what I'm going to do tomorrow."

He held her tighter.

"And I've just lied," she said to him.

"You lied?" She could hear the surprise in his voice.

"I *am* crying."

She knew she was getting his shirt wet with her tears, but once they started, she couldn't stop them. She cried out all the grief, all the anger, all the frustration, all the hurt, until finally her head ached.

She pulled back and said, shakily, "I need a handkerchief."

"Here, take mine."

She shook her head. "I have my own." She managed a weak smile. "These days, it doesn't do to be without, you know."

"I suppose."

His chest was so comfortable, she didn't want to leave the safe enclosure of his arms, and she leaned against him while she fished in her pocket for her handkerchief.

"Let's go for a walk," he suggested. "You can bring your hankie."

"Am I going to need it?"

"Only if the vision of a broken down barn brings you to tears."

She had no idea what he was talking about. She knew that he and her brothers had been pulling down the back barn, but why would he want her to go see it now?

Not that it mattered. She would have followed him to Timbuktu if he'd asked her.

He led her, holding her hand, out to the spot where they'd been working. Most of the outbuilding had been taken apart, and she saw the sure hand of her brother George in the neatness of the work site. The wood was piled in a tidy stack, the nails were contained in an old coffee tin, and the tools were out of sight, probably safely stowed in his toolbox in the barn.

"What do you see here?" he asked her, as he stood behind her, his hands on her shoulders.

"I see some trees and a sky and a back barn that, if you all had just waited a week or two, probably would have fallen down of its own accord."

He chuckled. "It was fairly awful."

"It was originally meant to store wagon equipment, but when we got the truck, George sold the horse and the wagon and its accoutrements, which is what he called the reins and the harness and all that. Big fancy word, but George likes fancy words."

Colin smiled as she continued, "Lately it's housed a skunk or two—I think you've already met one—and a possum, and batches and batches of field mice, and a hornets' nest every year."

"So it's the local zoo?"

"You could say that. It's a definite improvement having it come down. Now I won't have to worry about what tenant is going to come out and greet me as I walk by." She shuddered as an old memory resurfaced. "There was even a snake in there once. Nonvenomous, Bud said—as he waved it in my face, of course—but still scary."

"Ah, typical Bud. So you see an old barn that needed to come down—and it is, bit by bit—and what else do you see?"

"I see the wood and the nails. George, always the thrifty one, will never throw away something even as little as a nail. I've seen him pound one straight to use again in a fence or something."

"Do you know what I see?" he asked as his fingers tightened on her shoulders. "I see hope. I see a family that won't stop believing and trusting in the future, so much so that they'll take down an old building and make plans for a new one."

"But he started this earlier," Lolly began, "before we knew that we'd have to sell the farm."

Colin leaned in, so close to her that his breath tickled her ear. "Do you really think he hasn't known this for some time? That he hasn't been trying to find a way out of it? But more importantly, once he decided that he couldn't save the farm, he continued on with this. Do you know what we're going to do with this lumber?"

Her head was spinning, not only with what he was telling her, but the very fact that he was so close to her.

"He's going to build a new shed, a toolshed."

"He says that, but I think it's just talk," she answered.

"No, he's got the plans all drawn up and ready to go. And he's talking about how he can store his tools in it. Lolly, is this the voice of a man who's given up hope?"

She couldn't bear it any more. She was tired of trying to stay upbeat and positive, when it was clear to her that their options were not just limited, but gone.

She twisted out of his hold and turned to face him. "You say this over and over, but here's the truth. Unless someone comes up with a way to save this farm, it's done. We can talk about having faith and having hope and all those pretty words, but we're like Bruno with that bone. All the meat is gone. It's just a bone. We can chew on it and chew on it and chew on it, *but it's just a bone.*"

Her chest hurt so bad she thought it would split open. "I've lived here my whole life. My entire past is here. I have nothing else. Nothing! There isn't anything romantic about poverty, and I think you, of all people, should know that. Look at you, sent out on the road with only a change of clothes and a bedroll."

"But it was my choice."

"Choice! You really don't understand, do you? There isn't anything called 'choice' any longer! There isn't enough money here, and without money, Colin, all options are closed. If you can't pay for a place to live, then you're homeless. If you can't pay for food to eat, you're hungry. Where's the choice in that?"

She didn't even bother to swab away the tears that coursed down her cheeks freely. "They don't call it a depression because everybody's having such a swell time."

With those words, she turned and marched back into the house, hating the way her life had turned against her.

❧

He stood in the clearing, his hands still open as if at any moment she might walk back into his embrace. His ears still rang with her words, sharp and direct.

She was right. It was fine for him to mouth platitudes about keeping her faith and having trust and all that, but there was a time, he knew, to put some muscle behind the plow God had given him, just as the minister had said in the service on Sunday. He had to push it forward to make it work.

What could he do?

Bruno was snuffling around in the foundation of the old barn, and Colin kept a wary eye on him. He wasn't too fond of any of the animals that Lolly had mentioned, particularly snakes, and Bruno had already proven his talent at rousting animals from the shed with the skunk.

The dog pawed away a loose brick and picked something up in his teeth. Every muscle in Colin's body prepared for immediate flight as the mutt headed his way.

But it wasn't an animal. It was a notebook, rubbed over with dirt. The cover was partially ripped away, and it was, of course, damp with dog drool. He could see that Bruno had created his own stash of treasures—a sock, three feathers, a piece of rubber that must have been a tire, a bone, a gnawed candle, and of course, the notebook.

Bruno must have taken it from the house and brought it out to the barn and buried it.

Colin opened it and began to read.

It was a charming story, beautifully told. He understood immediately what he had in his hand.

It was Lolly's story.

ten

I thought my dreams were safe with him. And perhaps they are. But I have no idea where he has taken them. Across the ocean to enchanting Paris? To a mountaintop in exotic Asia? Into a pyramid in Egypt? I hope he takes good care of them, for these dreams are fragile things. And they are mine.

Dinner was a quiet meal, without much discussion.

George was angry with Bud, who was angry that George was angry. Lolly sighed. They'd been through this many times before. Eventually the whole thing would evaporate and life would go on as if nothing had ever happened.

It drove her crazy.

Colin seemed preoccupied. Occasionally he would lift his head and smile vaguely at her, and then lapse back into his own thoughts.

She shouldn't have snapped at him that afternoon. He was only trying to help, but she had reached the end of her patience. And she had to admit that nothing she said was untrue. It might have benefited from some editing of the tone, admittedly, but the facts themselves were indisputable.

He was probably hurt, and that unfocused smile was simply his way of dealing with her dreadful tirade. After dinner she'd try to catch some time with him alone and apologize. That would undoubtedly go a long way to heal his ruffled feathers.

She beamed happily at him, content with her decision, and let the dinner ride on in silence.

After the last noodle had been eaten, she cleared the table

and prepared to wash the dishes. Usually Colin helped her, but tonight he wasn't there, and bless his heart, she thought, who could blame him?

No, definitely an apology was in order. It wouldn't solve the problem of the farm, but at least her heart would be happier.

She hummed contentedly while she straightened the kitchen. She hung the dish towel so that the smiling teakettle she'd embroidered faced outward. The plates and cups and silverware were washed and dried and put away, and the counters wiped off.

With one last unnecessary pass at the immaculate stovetop, she took off her apron, looped it over the hook on the broom closet door, and retied her hair.

She took a deep breath and entered the living room. "Colin, I'm sor—"

Her toe caught on the edge of the throw rug, and she tripped. Everything slowed down so that she caught the entire fall in amazing detail: stumbling on the rug, splaying across a sleeping Bruno who barked sharply at her for interrupting his dog dreams, sliding across the floor on her knees and chin, and coming to a halt against the edge of the sofa.

"And that's why they call it a *throw* rug," Bud quipped as he sprang to help her up.

"Are you all right?" George said.

"You're bleeding." Bud held up his hand and showed her the smears.

"Is anything broken?" George held her elbow, steadying her.

"Just my pride."

"Oh, that," Bud said dismissively.

"Where's Colin?" she asked, as she finally realized that this had all been for naught, since he wasn't in the room.

"I don't know." George looked around, as if realizing for the first time that Colin wasn't there. "I don't know that he came in here after supper."

"He did, but then he went to his room in the old house," Bud volunteered. Then he leered at his sister. "Maybe he is your mail-order groom after all. Did you want to go for a long walk in the moonlight? A little hand-holding? Kissy-kissy? Smooch-smooch?"

With all the dignity she could muster, she left the room and went into her bedroom. There was no way she was going to get to talk to Colin, not while her brothers were around.

She didn't miss her notebook as much as she'd thought she would. She had the real thing here in her home.

She sprawled on her bed and let her mind wander to the subject she enjoyed the most—Colin.

If only this stupid depression hadn't interfered. He could have found work in Valley Junction, or even stayed and helped with the farm, freeing George to marry Ruth if he wished. Bud—well, she'd never figured out a solution for Bud. At some point he'd find a girl in the area and settle down. The problem with him was the settling down part.

She'd never thought she'd find love here and had long ago resigned herself to being a spinster and living out the rest of her days keeping Bud in line.

But now she had Colin. She loved him. She needed him.

What if he chooses to leave? Resolutely she tried to push the idea out of her mind, but it stayed just inside the fringes. There was no reason he should stay, and in fact, every reason for him to go.

He could take her with him.

Her brain began to play with the thought. They could go somewhere else.

Now that the farm was going to be sold, she had no reason to stay in Valley Junction. In fact, she would probably have to move and find a job. Of course her first thought was that she could go to St. Paul or Minneapolis, but why should she limit herself?

The economy was hurting there, too, but at least in a city they'd have a fighting chance at earning a living.

Perhaps this was a blessing in disguise. The cost was horrendous, but maybe there was a silver lining in this dark cloud.

She'd asked for this, longed for this, ached for this, and now she had it.

Freedom.

She laced her fingers behind her head and lay back on the pillow and stared at the ceiling. The more she played out the scenario in her mind, the more she liked it. Yes, it was absolutely possible.

She and Colin would move to the city.

George and Ruth could take the profit from the farm—assuming anyone would buy it—and start again, here or somewhere else.

And Bud? He was the wild card in the lot, but she knew even that would resolve itself.

God would help her sort this all out. He didn't create problems that His people couldn't solve.

With those plans floating through her mind like butterflies, she fell asleep.

&

The sun hadn't come up yet, but he couldn't wait. Once again he rolled up two blankets with rope and stowed a change of clothes and his Bible in his backpack.

In this hour before sunrise, the farm was silent except for the last sounds of the night birds calling to each other from the cottonwoods. The chickens were tucked in the coop, sleeping soundly in their straw nests.

Bruno sprang to his feet, his nails scrabbling across the kitchen linoleum as Colin tiptoed through the room.

Colin knelt and scratched the dog's head. "Take care of them for me, will you please? Especially Lolly."

He stood up and surveyed the room where he'd spent so many enjoyable hours with Lolly, falling in love with her as she peeled the carrots that never seemed to grow completely, or as she stood over a basin full of soapy water and dishes, her hair that couldn't stay in place escaping into those eyes as dark as wet granite.

Every part of his being screamed at him: *Stay!* His heart spoke the loudest.

But he couldn't. He needed to leave, to go back to where he'd begun.

He had work to do.

His heart wanted to stay here, tucked in the curve of the Minnesota River, where within a couple of weeks the first gilt of autumn would touch the landscape. He wanted to sit on the pier with Lolly, enjoying October crisp mornings when the sun was as golden as the leaves, against a backdrop of clear blue sky.

And then to watch the first snowflakes fall. . .together. To stand in the warmth of the farmhouse and watch the winter put on an icy mantle, or to walk in the snow, their footsteps marking where they had been, and only their love deciding where they should go.

To await spring with its burst of brilliant new green, the first shoots of life to appear after the winterkill on the land.

He sighed. It was not to be.

He'd come in search of God, in search of meaning, and he had found it. He realized at last that it was very simple.

All he'd had to do was open his heart and let God bloom. God had been there all along. He had just been waiting.

He shifted his backpack onto his shoulders and settled the bedroll.

This was so difficult to do.

And so necessary.

"Good-bye, Lolly," he said into the dark. "God bless you."

With that, he turned and left the house, shutting the door very quietly behind him, and walked down the road, headed toward the future.

❧

The chickens squawked and clucked and complained loudly, and Lolly smiled as she tied her apron on. Colin had probably just walked by. The silly birds had decided that whenever he appeared, it was time for him to feed them.

And, soft touch that he was, he almost always did, even if it was only a few kernels as a treat.

She went to the window to call him in for morning coffee. It was weak, to be sure, but it was coffee.

The chickens, though, weren't being fed. Instead, they were milling around anxiously, pecking at the bare ground as if that would make the food appear.

Where was Colin?

Bud slid into the kitchen with his usual carelessness, and she automatically chided him. "Can't you just walk into a room? You know, one foot in front of the other like a normal person?"

"Aw, Lolly, you know I don't do imitations." He picked up a cup and poured from the coffeepot. "I thought we were having coffee now."

"We are."

"So what is this?"

"Coffee."

"No, I mean really. What is it?"

She sighed. "It's coffee."

"Coffee is brown. This isn't brown. It's beige."

"I had to make it a little bit weak."

George joined them at that moment. "Any coffee left?"

Bud hooted. "Depends on what you call 'coffee.' There's some stuff left that Lolly brewed up, but it's a stretch to call it coffee."

George poured himself a cup. "It is kind of, well, transparent, Lolly."

"I'm trying to make it stretch until I can get into town with some more eggs."

"So what do you suppose is better, brother of mine," Bud asked as he pulled a chair out from the table and sat backwards on it, "five cups of weak coffee, or two cups of good coffee?"

"I don't know, Bud." George dished up scrambled eggs from the skillet and joined him at the table, but with his chair facing forward. "You tell me, as I'm sure you will."

"Sounds like somebody got up on the wrong side of the bed today."

Bud was in one of his taunting moods, Lolly realized. That was going to make the day all that much more difficult. When he was like this, especially first thing in the morning, it set the tone for George, who liked to eat his breakfast in grumpy silence.

"Where's Colin?" George asked, interrupting Bud's discussion of coffee.

"I don't know," Lolly said, frowning at her own cup of coffee. Maybe she had been a bit too light-handed with the ground beans. This looked a lot more like tea. She took an experimental sip. It tasted like hot water with a faint aroma of coffee. "Isn't he with you?"

"I haven't seen him," George said.

"Me, either."

"Those fool chickens are about to drive me insane, too," George said, sending a dark look in the general direction of the henhouse. "Colin needs to get up and feed them."

It wasn't like Colin to ignore the chickens, Lolly thought. Something was wrong.

"Would one of you do me a favor and check the old house?"

"Why?" Bud asked as he reached over to George's plate and speared a forkful of eggs.

"Get your own!" George growled.

"It's easier to just eat off yours," Bud said.

"Stop!" Lolly came around the corner of the counter. "Just stop it, please! You two don't need to argue about every little thing that comes your way. I want one of you to go check on Colin and—"

She frowned as an ominous crunch behind her broke into her rant. "Bruno, you didn't!"

"Oh, he did," Bud said.

The dog had gotten into the garbage and pulled out the eggshells and was contentedly munching away on them.

"Nasty dog!" She leaned down and forced Bruno's jaws open and pulled out what she could of the shells. "Now you'll probably get sick."

She cleaned up the shells that were spilled on the floor, and when she stood up, George was standing beside her.

His face was solemn. "Lolly, Colin's not in his room."

"He's probably out in the back somewhere." She dropped the shells back into the garbage. "Bad dog!" she said, shaking her finger at Bruno. "No more garbage!"

"Lolly, I think he's gone."

"Gone?"

She froze, her finger still pointed at the dog.

"Gone. His bed is made, and his pack and bedroll are gone."

How could he be gone? How could he? She braced herself against the counter with both hands. "He's gone?"

George nodded. "I'm sorry. Sis, I'm really sorry."

"He's just outside somewhere. He can't have left."

"Lolly, he's gone."

"Then there's a note. Let's look for a note."

"No note. I already checked."

"Why would he leave? Why wouldn't he stay? He'll be back. He will. You just wait and see."

He didn't say anything. But she saw the answer in his eyes.

Whatever was left of her world shattered. She turned around and slammed her fist into the countertop. "This is not fair! Not fair!"

"Lolly. . ." George tried to put his arm around her, but she shook it off.

"First God takes both Mom and Dad and leaves us here on the farm. Then He brings a drought to the land, and if that's not enough, a depression, too. My name gets smeared all across Valley Junction—"

"Actually," Bud interjected, "that was my fault. Not God's."

"Whatever. He could have stopped you. He could have tripped you when you were reaching for that blanket for the governor rooster. He could have had George run over a nail and get a flat tire. He could have made you decide that for once you'd keep your mouth shut."

"Eleanor Ann Prescott!" George barked. "No more!"

"And He could have let Colin stay here."

The rage in Lolly dissipated, and she slid down to the floor. "I'm out of fight. I can't go on anymore. We don't have enough money for even a halfway decent cup of coffee today. What are we going to do for dinner tomorrow?"

"We have the chickens," Bud said.

"We can't eat eggs forever," she pointed out.

"Not just the eggs," George said.

"Oh, this is exactly what I mean! If we eat the chickens,

there won't be any more eggs. Do you see? I'm sorry I yelled at God. I am. But I just don't know what to do."

"We aren't totally out of options," George said. "In Mankato—"

"I want to be here. I want to be here with Colin."

"Well," Bud said, "I know what I'm going to do. I'm going to find Colin and make him answer to me, that's what I'm going to do."

"You're right, you know that, little brother? We saved that fellow's life! We did!" George pushed back his plate angrily. "We saved his life, and we took him into our home, and we fed him, and gave him clothes, and let our sister fall in love, and—"

What were they saying?

Lolly raised her head. "Wait just a second. You let me fall in love? Are you both insane? I think I can fall in love on my own, thank you very much."

"But he told us that he told you that he loved you," Bud said.

"He told you that, did he?" Cold fury was beginning to displace hurt. "What else did he tell you about us?"

Bud screwed his face into a thoughtful frown. "Well, George asked him if he'd kissed you, and—"

"You did *not*!" She nearly flew to her feet. "Tell me you didn't do that."

"Well, I might have." George at least had the good grace to look uncomfortable.

"And what did he say?"

"He didn't really say anything. He didn't seem to be a kiss-and-tell kind of guy."

Lolly snorted. "More like a kiss-and-leave kind of guy."

George pushed his chair back with force. "So he did. He did kiss you."

She put her hands over her forehead. What on earth had

she done to deserve this from her brothers? Wasn't anything going to go her way?

"I am going to find a place no one will bother me for a while," she said, with as much dignity as she could muster. "I need to be alone for a while. But first I am going to feed the chickens."

She straightened her apron, tucked her hair back into the bun, and left the room. Her brothers' words carried through the open doorway.

"Which way do you suppose he went?"

"If we take the back road, we can probably catch him before he gets to Mankato."

"Unless he's going west. But why would he go west?"

"He's from New York. He's wending his sorry way back there."

"But he was going west when we found him."

"Well, it's heading into winter. He'll probably want to go home."

"Let's do the back road."

"We'll find him and bring him back here and make him marry Lolly."

That was entirely too much.

She spun on her heel and turned back into the kitchen. "Don't do me any favors. I don't want him."

Bud narrowed his eyes. "But we do, Lolly. Boy, do we ever!"

❧

Colin saw the truck as it came down the road, and he ducked into the underbrush, rolling down a slight embankment as he lost his balance with the pack and bedroll strapped to his back. He could easily see Lolly's brothers in the front of the truck. From the way Bud was leaning out the window, scanning the sides of the road, and the forward thrust of George's chin as he hunkered over the steering wheel, it was clear they knew he was gone—and they were furious.

He couldn't blame them. But this was a way for them to weather the situation, and as difficult as it was, he had to leave. They had given him his life back. He owed them this much.

The last missing bits of his life had all come together, and with them, the answer.

It would work. It had to.

eleven

Farewell. It means, literally, travel safely. Be healthy. Enjoy your trip. And don't forget about the one who loves you, the one who stays behind, holding her heart in her hands because it doesn't fit inside her any more. Farewell. Go with my love.

Lolly and her brothers rode into Valley Junction Sunday morning. Without Colin in the truck, the three of them were able to sit without being crammed together. Lolly held her own Bible now, one that she'd gotten from her parents when she passed her confirmation class. The days of sharing Colin's Bible were gone.

As soon as she stepped out of the truck, Hildegard Hopper hobbled toward the truck in shoes that were clearly too small for her. Her feet bulged over the tops of them, and she winced with each step. Lolly had to admit that they were beautiful, though. Made of a soft shell pink leather with a pearl fan on each toe, they must have cost a fortune. *Or at least a month's grocery bill,* Lolly thought a bit jealously.

Amelia Kramer followed in Hildegard's wake like a small, drab rowboat. Her eyes were bright with anticipation, and both women smiled toothily.

"Why, Eleanor," Hildegard said, and Lolly flinched, "I see it's just the three of you today."

"Yes, it is."

"We left the dog at home," Bud said.

Lolly pinched his side so hard he yelped, and he looked at

145

her with a fake wide-eyed innocence that she was sure didn't fool the two women for a moment. "Why did you do that? It's true. Bruno's at home. So it's just you, George, and me."

"Do you know why I like you so much, Bud?" Hildegard asked, as Amelia nodded enthusiastically behind her.

"We really like you," Amelia echoed.

Why do they call him Bud, and me Eleanor? Lolly wondered. *They must not know that his real name is—*

She suppressed the thought, realizing that it might actually have some bargaining power with her brother. She could threaten to tell the two women what his real name was. Bud hated it and wouldn't let anyone use it.

"Why do you like Bud so much?" she asked, wanting to deflect their attention onto her much more worthy brother.

"He is just so cute and so clever," Hildegard said, beaming at him. "And such a good boy, coming to church every Sunday."

"Very good boy," Amelia repeated.

"All three of the Prescotts come every week, don't they, Amelia?" Hildegard asked.

"They do."

"But for a while they had someone else with them, if I'm not mistaken."

Amelia took a step closer.

If the woman had antennae like a beetle, I'm sure they'd be wiggling like mad, Lolly thought as she took a corollary step back.

"A man, Hildegard," Amelia contributed. "A man, named Collier? Colbert? Something like that?"

"You know exactly what his name was," Bud said.

"Oh my, do I now?" Hildegard touched her fingertip to her mouth in artificial coyness. "What was the name of Lolly's mail-order groom? Oh! I wasn't supposed to mention that, was I? Silly me."

"His name was Quincy," Bud said. "Quincy Peapod Featherbee the Third."

Lolly almost choked. She pinched him again, but he ignored her warning and plunged on ahead.

"Yes, Quincy, or QPF the Third as we liked to call him, was a splendid fellow. Sailed in one day on a clipper ship, right on the Minnesota River, it was, and stopped for tea. His ship, sadly, sailed without him, but they finally realized he was missing and they came back for him. We miss him terribly, especially his strawberry and cream cheese sandwiches. Now, if you'll excuse us, it's time for worship."

Bud took Lolly's left elbow, and George took her right, and together they walked into the church.

When they were seated, Lolly scolded her brother in a whisper. "What on earth was that about? Now it'll be even worse. I thought that everyone had let the mail-order groom thing pass, and now this. We'll be the laughing stock of the town."

Then she turned to George. "And you! You just stood there like a big old goose and didn't say a word! What's the matter with you?"

"I didn't hear you say anything," he pointed out.

"Well, I didn't, but I was pinching him." She settled in her seat, her back straight and her hands folded over her purse.

"Oh, well, that makes all the difference in the world," George said. "You were pinching him."

"Is that a bit of sarcasm I hear?"

"It's a lot of sarcasm." He leaned closer. "Don't you see the method in his madness? What do you suppose the chances of us being corralled by those two again, either here or at our house? I think he might have just finished it."

"Or finished us," Lolly said.

She only half-listened to the sermon, paid a bit of attention to the hymns, and listlessly followed the readings. She was tired. Tired of constantly fighting with her brothers, fighting with Hildegard and Amelia, tired of fighting the constant lack of money, tired of fighting loneliness and hopelessness. Just tired.

Once again she was trapped, trapped without options, without choices. Without hope.

As they were leaving the church, she felt a touch on her arm. It was Dr. Greenleigh, the man who had first examined Colin.

"I don't see your young man with you today," the doctor said.

"First off, I don't think he's my young man," Lolly retorted.

"Fair enough. I was just concerned because he's always here with you at services." Dr. Greenleigh's friendly face creased with a frown, and Lolly reproached herself for being so rude.

"Actually, he's gone again." The words came out smoothly, and she congratulated herself on how normal they sounded.

"Oh, good. So you did exactly the right thing, provided the correct amount of care, and got him healthy again. To be honest, I had my doubts at first that he would survive."

She drew back in shock. "You did? But you didn't say anything."

"You know," he said, "as a doctor I get to see a lot that surprises me. People who should by all rights be dead from an injury will live and you'd never know they'd had any kind of trauma. Of course, I see the other way, too, when death is unexpected."

"That's true enough, I suppose," she answered.

"But that's taught me the greatest lesson ever. I didn't read it in a medical book or hear it in a lecture. No, I learned it from my patients. And do you know what that lesson is?"

She shook her head.

"It's that you can never underestimate the power of the human spirit, of its desire to live and soar as close to the angels as it can. That, I suspect, is what healed the man who collapsed on your property."

"It was the strength of his soul," she said almost to herself. "That's it, isn't it?"

"Don't discount the role of support. Just like when you might need someone's arm to lean on when you're walking on an icy stretch, that's very important for survival. Without you, he probably would have died. You were the support he needed." He patted her on the arm. "You were the hands of God."

She stood in the shadow of the church, mulling over what he had said, and she kept coming up against something. She didn't much like the way she had been acting since Colin left. Her words were snappish, and her patience was short while her anger was long.

She needed to guard her heart, that much was common sense, but she didn't need to encase it in cement and then make everyone around her suffer because it hurt. She was focusing on the wrong thing.

She had done what she needed to. Colin was alive because of her.

Take the victory, she told herself. *You didn't lose. You won. Take the victory.*

༜

Colin was out of practice. He'd lost his ability to duck around rail yard guards and hide behind boxcars. He'd managed most of his travels from New York City by bartering rides when his feet had given out and he wasn't able to walk anymore. He'd do some cleaning up for the yardmaster in exchange for the man's silence about his presence in the boxcar.

But not all yardmasters were amenable to this, and out of necessity he'd developed an ability to find an empty railway car in the dark to sleep in, and if it had taken him farther along on his destination, so much the better. At first it hadn't bothered him. It was one more exciting step in the life he'd taken on that fateful day when he left his home.

He remembered how, as the days wore on and the thrill wore thin, he spent long hours debating the rights and wrongs of what he was doing. Riding the rails, he told himself, was the hobo's life. That's what they did. But on the other hand, it didn't seem right to tag along without paying in some fashion, even if the ride was in a dusty closed car.

He wasn't going to do that this time. It had been too early in the day to reach anyone in New York to see if some money could be wired to him.

If only he had waited longer. He'd chased sleep all night, until he'd made his decision to leave in the early trickle of morning light. His impetuosity had put him back on the rails. He had no choice except to go back, at least part of the way, the same way he'd come out, as a vagabond.

Still, when he got to Minneapolis he'd try to contact his company in New York. Let them know he was alive. Tell them he was all right. Ask for money.

He smiled wryly as he thought of the reaction that call would bring. Would they even believe him?

Night fell earlier in September than it had in June when he came out to Minnesota, and his judgment was off on which train went where and when—because now he was going in the opposite direction.

He climbed into an empty boxcar and curled up in the corner. Once he got some sleep, he'd probably figure this out.

This wasn't at all the same trip. He'd heard some talk in the railway station in Mankato of cold moving through. It would probably chase him all the way to the East Coast.

This time of year, the temperatures and precipitation could

be unpredictable. It often swung from the shirtsleeves of summer warmth to the first cold breath of winter—within a day or two.

"You going far?" A voice spoke from the opposite corner of the boxcar, and he realized he wasn't alone. It was so completely dark in the boxcar that he hadn't even noticed someone else sharing the space with him.

"To New York City. What about you?"

"I want to go someplace warm for winter. I'd like to see Virginia. Tennessee. Louisiana. And Florida. Oh, I'd like to go to Florida someday. Wait, I got a picture to show you." Some scuffling in the vicinity of the voice followed, and a match scratched into light, revealing a man with a heavy growth of beard, his glasses taped together, and wearing a red plaid flannel shirt that was more hole than cloth. He lit the stub end of a candle with the match and scuttled over toward Colin. "See this?"

He handed Colin a postcard of a palm tree on a shoreline. A couple played volleyball while the sun shone off a pristine sand beach and the turquoise-tinted water. "Don't it look like a place a fella should be? And look. See? On the back. There's writing. It says *Dear Grandpa, Come to Florida and we will get seashells. I love you. Imogene.* She wrote that herself, my Imogene did."

The card was addressed to Grady Shields, General Delivery, Omaha, Nebraska. "It's really lovely, and your granddaughter strikes me as a charming girl. So your name's Grady, is it?"

The man sat back on his haunches. "How did you know that?"

"It says so right here." Colin pointed to the address and Grady nodded.

"Oh, right. I'd forgotten about that."

The man couldn't read. Colin had figured that out when

the words weren't exactly the same as what he'd said. The gist was the same, but the words were different enough to clue him in to the fact that Grady might be illiterate. The actual words were, *Dear Grandpa, You can come to Florida and we can find seashells. I love you. Imogene.*

"Does this train go to Florida?" Colin weighed the advisability of trusting a man who couldn't read.

Grady shook his head. "Nope. Goes to Chicago and then heads off toward Indianapolis and on to Nashville."

"Nashville is south."

"My Imogene isn't in Nashville."

The cars shuddered a bit as the train came to life, ready for its travels, and Grady blew out the candle. "Just in case," he said cryptically.

As the train rattled its way out of the station, Colin asked, over the grind of the wheels, "When did you last see Imogene?"

"Oh, I'd say going on four years now. I've had this card for about two of those four. It's as precious to me as my own blood."

Colin closed his eyes as the motion of the train hypnotically swayed him back and forth in a regular rhythm. "Are you a Christian, Grady?" he asked at last.

"Why, yes indeed, I am. I count myself among those who love the Lord, yes I do."

"Do you know the Lord's Prayer?"

"Yes, I do."

"The Twenty-third Psalm?"

"That's *The Lord is my shepherd*, ain't it?"

"It is. Do you know it by heart?"

"Parts of it but not all of it. Why are you asking all these questions? You planning to put me on the stage in some Sunday school pageant? Dress me up in a bathrobe and have me be one of the Wise Men? Want me to sing 'Jesus Loves Me,' too?" Grady's rusty laugh echoed in the empty boxcar.

Colin joined in the laughter. It felt good to laugh with Grady.

"The reason I'm asking," he clarified, "is that I'm thinking you might be wanting to perk up your reading skills before you get to Imogene's house, am I right?"

There was a long silence from Grady, and Colin feared he'd offended him. Then Grady spoke. "I can't read at all. Not even a single word. I was raised on a farm back in the olden days, as Imogene calls them, and we got a little bit of schooling but not much. I can cipher a tad, but reading was one of those school subjects that just didn't stick in this poor brain."

"You can't read at all?"

"Not a word, not a syllable, not a letter. Oh, I ain't proud of that, let me tell you, no sirree, but facts is facts, and the fact here is that I just couldn't learn."

Colin was grateful for the darkness. He didn't know if Grady would speak so freely in the daylight. "How do you know which train to get on, then? Do you ask? Don't you run the risk of them getting suspicious?"

"*Pffft*. Most of the rail yard people don't care as long as you're neat and tidy and don't leave a mess in the car for them to clean up. Like me, for example. Tidy Grady. Nobody bothers me because I also help them when I can."

"One hand watches the other." Colin smiled in the inky train car.

"Huh?"

"Oh, just something a dear friend told me."

"How dear are we talking about?" Grady asked.

"Very dear."

"And you're going home to her now?"

"No. I've got some things to do before I can ask her to settle in with me."

"Don't wait too long," Grady advised. "Hearts change."

Colin didn't answer. It was his greatest fear, and it, more than anything, would keep him away.

He changed the subject, this time to the conditions at the various railroad stations, and as Grady talked, he put his head back and thought about how his life had taken yet another odd twist. Here he was, once again, riding in boxcars, he who had less than a year ago been driven wherever he wanted to go.

But now he had a new idea, how to make this time on the rails truly blessed. The phone call to New York could wait. This was more important. He had work to do in that boxcar.

&

"Here."

Bud tossed something to her when he walked in the door. It landed on the counter and slid across the length, nearly knocking over the cup of tea she'd just made and landing at her feet.

She bent over and picked it up.

It was a new notebook. This one had pink roses scaling a trellis on the off-white cover. And in the middle it said, *Mankato Hotel.*

"Very pretty, Bud. Thanks!" She tucked it into her pocket. She'd have to think about this, using a new notebook. What was that old adage? Once burned, twice shy? It certainly fit this scenario.

"Well, aren't you going to ask me what I'm doing with a notebook from the Mankato Hotel? Aren't you even a little bit curious? Don't you want to know if I went to Mankato, and how I got there, and what I did? And why I ended up at the hotel there?"

"Actually," she said with a smile, "I didn't even know you were gone."

"Okay, I wasn't gone. I didn't go to Mankato. But I saw this notebook at the post office, and I said that I had a sister who sure liked to write romantic stuff down and the fellow gave it to me. Then we got to talking, and he said I could come to Mankato and he'd see about getting me some work. So I didn't go yet, but I am going to."

"Really, Bud?" Something somewhere in the area of her heart ached with a sudden heavy burden. "You want to move to Mankato?"

He wrapped his body around a chair in a motion that, if she'd tried it, would have caused severe damage to her hips and torso. "I don't want to, but this poverty stuff is about to make me loony. I love this place as much as you do, but we can't do it, sis. We just can't."

She leaned across the counter, her hands cradled around her hot cup of tea. "I know."

In a rare show of brotherly affection, he patted her arm. "You know that he'll find you no matter where you are, don't you?"

He had, with that single sentence and the unnamed pronoun, identified yet another basis for her not wanting to leave. As irrational as it might be—Colin hadn't given any indication that he'd be coming back—her heart still clung to the awkward hope.

How *would* he find her if she went with her brothers somewhere else? It wasn't like she could exactly leave a note on the door for him.

She missed him terribly. The thought of going through life without him was depressing for her to consider.

Bruno padded over to lie at her feet, a half-eaten shoe hanging from his jaws. Grateful for the change in focus, she asked her brother, "Do you suppose that there's a chance our dog is part goat?"

"I think he's kind of lonely," he answered. "Think about it."

"Oh, because Colin's gone?"

"Never mind him. I think he misses Hildegard Hopper and Amelia Kramer and their shoes!"

twelve

I can't forget him, and when I sleep, I find him. We run through frosted fields, leaving copper footprints on the silvered landscape. Always we hold hands, as if that will keep us together when this earthly sphere drives us apart. Our fingers are locked together in an endless lover's knot, now and forever. I can't let go.

The grasses were crisping, and ice had begun to creep along the edges of the river in sheltered areas. In the waters along the edge, crystal touched fallen leaves, and the world glittered its way into winter.

Lolly walked down to the pier by herself. They were moving out the next week, into Mankato, where George and Bud had both found small jobs work, George as a handyman at the teachers college and Bud as a busboy at the hotel restaurant. Neither job offered more than a day-to-day offer of employment, but, as Bud said, that was better than a poke in the eye.

She'd go along with them. Perhaps she could clean houses or work as a cook's assistant.

And the farm would stay right where it was, but there wouldn't be anyone in it to love it. George had figured out more numbers and come up with what he called the If Budget. *If* he and Bud worked at least six days out of every week, and *if* they were paid promptly, and *if* the apartment he'd found was all right, and *if* the cost of everything stayed right where it was at the moment, they could keep the farm.

There were more *if*s, but Lolly's head spun with this short list.

There was one more *if* on his list. It was the big one. *If* the nation's economy didn't get any worse. That was the one item that drove everything else.

She didn't want to leave the farm. It was everything to her. Her entire life had been spent on the land, and the river that flowed through it was like her own blood.

Thanksgiving was coming up, and then Christmas, and the thought of spending those holidays in a tiny apartment made her heart sink. She'd asked George about the possibility of at least coming out to the farm for the holidays, and he'd thought about it and decided that if there was enough money to put gasoline in the truck and enough wood stored at the farm to heat the house with the fireplace, then yes, they could.

It was a small sparkle, but it was good. Bud had been chopping firewood all week, without his usual snappish commentaries, so she knew it was important to him, too.

The house was packed, for the most part. The crystal vase was cradled in layers of blankets and would ride to Mankato on Lolly's lap, and the housewares had been divided between the two homes. The furniture was staying at the farm because the apartment was furnished and taking the sagging old tapestry couch wouldn't be worth it, assuming it would even make the trip without falling apart.

The apartment was small. One bedroom with a curtain dividing it from the rest of the place. Privacy was available only in the cramped bathroom. The first time she'd seen the tiny room, Lolly had stood in the doorway, amazed at the way the sink, bathtub, toilet, and a cabinet dovetailed into the space that effectively.

The kitchen, which George had tried to tell her was

efficient—"Look, you don't even have to move! From one spot you can reach the stove, the ice box, the cabinets, and the sink!"—was dark but clean. They gave her the bedroom and with an elaborate arrangement of one brother on the couch and one on a pallet on the floor, with a rotating schedule of who got the couch and who was forced to sleep on the floor, they took the living room. Bruno, of course, got his choice. He was too big to argue with.

Again, it was Bud who summed it up best. "The nice thing about living in a depression is that we don't have anything, so this fits us just perfect!"

Mankato was interesting, but she did not want to leave the farm, especially now when all around her, the change of the season was in full bore, the trees now in resplendent crimson, elegant gold, and fiery auburn.

At least this was, for the moment, still hers, and as long as things went the way George had outlined them, she would still be able to come to the farm.

The sun had melted the early morning frost, leaving the pier dark with moisture. She stepped out on it and sat on the edge and remembered the day they all went fishing and Bruno caught the catfish. On this pier, Colin had kissed her for the very first time.

And on this pier, he had kissed her for the very last time.

She didn't write in the notebook that Bud had brought her. She'd tried, but her fingers would freeze up when she opened to a new page. Now the story ran only in her mind, and there were times when it was all that kept her going.

❧

Each night, Colin and Grady leaned over Colin's Bible. As they would say the familiar words of the Lord's Prayer or the Twenty-third Psalm, they would follow along on the page, matching word for sound. And when they tired of that, with a short piece of a pencil, Colin taught Grady the letters for his name.

"I'm going to learn this for Imogene," Grady said. "If it's all right with you, I'll ride with you until I get this in my brain. I have to do this for my Imogene."

One cold afternoon, Colin and Grady took refuge in the station in Pittsburgh. Colin found an abandoned newspaper and spread it out in front of them.

"Let's do the headline together," he said. "'PRESIDENT. ROOSEVELT. VISITS...'"

Grady stood and paced nervously and then sat back down.

"Something under your skin?" Colin asked curiously as his new friend fidgeted.

"I'm tired of living like this, always on the move. I want to find a place, settle down, maybe try the family thing again." Grady touched his chest pocket where Colin knew the postcard from his granddaughter was. "I've let too many people go unloved. That's wrong, and I've got to make it right. It's been good knowing you, and thank you for trying to teach this old grizzled head how to read. At the very least, I can read some of the Bible."

"You don't have a Bible, do you?" Colin asked; and when Grady shook his head no, Colin reached into his pack and pulled out his. "Here, take this."

"You're giving me your Bible?" Grady looked at Colin in surprise.

It was the Bible that had been given to him when he'd been on the road before and so in need of the Word, and now, it seemed right to pass it on to another traveler who would also benefit.

"Are you sure?" Grady asked. "I'd be honored to carry it, knowing how it came into your possession."

"I'm sure. Here, let's do this."

They opened the Bible, and under the name Colin Hammett, the new owner wrote in labored but proud letters, *Grady Shields*.

Bible in hand, Grady touched his fingers to his forehead, turned, and was lost in the crowd.

Colin watched him go, sending a prayer with him. *Pad his footsteps with peace. Reunite him with love.*

He looked at the posted schedule board. If he hurried, he could slip out and catch the next train to New York City.

It was amazing, he thought as he settled himself in for the long ride, how someone who'd come into his life for such a brief time had given him direction. People like Grady were truly gifts.

He must have been truly exhausted, for when he awoke, the train was slowing down, pulling into the yard. He yawned and stretched, and when he stepped out, a familiar cityscape surrounded him.

Pulling his pack and bedroll onto his back, he headed for the neighborhood he knew so well.

It was quite a long walk, but he jogged along happily. It was good to be home.

At last he came to the building where his apartment was. The doorman stopped him. "You have business here?"

"I live here."

"We don't have bums living here. Go peddle your papers elsewhere!" The doorman lifted his whistle, ready to call for police assistance.

"No, I live here. I'm Colin Hammett."

"Mr. Hammett disappeared—oh, sir!" The doorman's face split into a wide beam, and Colin could tell he had stopped just short of hugging him. "It's good to have you back. My, you're looking a bit, well—"

"Ragged?" Colin laughed. "Just let me in so I can bathe and shave and change my clothes. Oh, it's so good to be home!"

His apartment hadn't changed at all. The maid service had come in and cleaned regularly, and even fresh towels were laid out in the bathroom. It was obvious that they had been ready for him to come back at any moment.

Within an hour, he was comfortable again and ready to head off to his office.

The doorman called for a driver, and as Colin rode the once-again familiar road to his business, he realized how truly changed he was. The people on the streets, hurrying toward their jobs or home after a day of labor, or those who had no employment and were going door to door, office to office, seeking anything—they now were real to him.

The office staff fell silent when he entered the room. And then, pandemonium broke loose. "Mr. Hammett is back!"

His cousin, Ralph, came out of the main office. "Colin!" The two embraced and then, after speaking to the staff and shaking hands with each one, Colin followed his cousin into the inner office.

"Where have you been? What happened?" his cousin began as they sat on opposite sides of his desk.

"I've been living in Minnesota after having my memory erased on a fence post. That's the short version," Colin said.

"The short version?" Ralph raised his eyebrows. "How much time should I set aside for the long version? This sounds like a story I want to hear."

"And it's a story I want to tell."

Ralph leaned across the desk. "What happened, Colin? Why did you leave so suddenly? One afternoon you simply came in here, told me you were off in search of yourself. You didn't contact me at all to let me know you were all right. Do you have any idea how worried I was? How worried we all were?"

"I'm sorry. It was thoughtless of me." Colin rubbed his forehead. "I'm so sorry."

"I think you should begin that long story now. I think I deserve it."

Night was darkening the sky in the window behind Ralph by the time Colin finished.

Ralph leaned back, his fingers laced behind his head. "Of course we want to help them. But what can we do, short of sending them money, which I'm glad to do."

Colin reached into his pocket and pulled out Lolly's notebook. "Take a look at this and tell me what you think."

His cousin opened it and began to scan it. Soon, though, he was reading in earnest, and at last, he put it down in front of him. "Amazing. Who is this writer?"

"She's the woman who saved me, and she is as incredible as her writing."

"Can we get her?"

"Let's talk, Ralph," Colin said.

When he left two hours later, night had wrapped the city in darkness, punctuated by the bright stars of streetlights and marquees, and he had a thick envelope in his hand and a smile on his face. Two days after that, he was at the Grand Central Terminal buying a ticket—destination, Minnesota. This time, there was no bedroll, no backpack.

❧

"It's good to be back here again," Bud said as he laid another log on the fire. "I've missed this old farm."

"It is nice, isn't it?" George sat down on the couch, sinking down as the cushions sagged.

"I like being able to move my arms like this," Lolly swung them around in crazy windmills. "I can't do that in the apartment without taking out a window or pulling down a towel rack or knocking the pictures off the wall."

"There's no time like Thanksgiving to come home," George said. "I look at these doors and these shelves and these walls and I think, my parents did this, with their own hands."

They didn't speak for a while. This was probably going to be the last time they'd gather like this at the farm.

The If Budget hadn't worked out. The jobs that George and Bruno had were too irregularly scheduled, and they simply didn't make enough money. Plus the rent on the tiny apartment was going up.

They needed cash, and the only way they could see to do it was to put the farm on the market. It might sell, or it might not.

For Lolly, either way was a nightmare.

"Good dinner," George said.

Bruno raised his head and dropped it again, as if the effort to move were too great. He'd shared the meal with them, including two of the cobs from the corn that Lolly caught him trying to escape with.

"I'm tired of chicken," Bud complained, but Lolly wasn't in the mood to argue with him. Of course he was tired of chicken. That was all they could afford.

They'd had to sell her chickens when they moved into town, and the farm was remarkably quiet without the hens and the rooster constantly squawking and crowing.

"I could stay here forever," George said from the depths of the sofa.

"Of course you could, " Bud shot back. "You can't get out of it. It's kind of like a conversation with Hildegard and Amelia."

They had just started to laugh when they heard a car pull up and a knock on the door.

"Oh no!" Bud said. "They're here!"

"Lolly, get rid of them," George said.

"You get rid of them," she told him. "Why do I always have to do it?"

"Because I can't get up, that's why."

She sighed and went to the door, mentally composing lines of conversation that would encourage the two women to leave.

Whatever would have possessed them to come on a holiday evening?

She opened the door and screamed as the snowy figure grabbed her and swung her around and around and around.

Bud tore into the room, with Bruno hot on his heels, a treasured corncob in his teeth.

Bud yelled and Bruno barked as Lolly cried and laughed and cried some more.

George, finally motivated to extricate himself from the couch, joined them and boomed, "Colin!" He stood, and with his arms crossed over his chest and his heavy sweater, he looked as formidable as a prizefighter. "At last. Now, come in and explain yourself."

Bud stood beside him, his hands jammed onto his waist. "You owe us at least that," he growled. "You owe Lolly that."

"Can't you see he's been traveling?" Lolly said. "Let him get his bearings again, and then you two can start grilling him. I have a few questions for him myself."

Finally, with a cup of warm tea in his hands and them all gathered in the kitchen around the table, he told them the story of finding the notebook and taking it to the publishing company.

"Apparently Bruno felt you weren't feeding him enough tires and feathers and books and such, so he'd started his own treasure chest of gastronomical delights out there where the back barn was. That's where I found your notebook, Lolly."

"My notebook?" Lolly asked, feeling dull but very happy.

"Your notebook. Bruno buried it where we took down the barn. He had quite the collection there. I know you'll be delighted to know that your notebook ranked right up there with some feathers and a sock and a chewed candle stub in his doggy mind."

"Oh, my." Lolly looked at the dog that was now happily licking the snow off Colin's boots. "He had it."

"He did. So I left here—"

Remembered pain washed over her. "Why did you just leave like that? Didn't you know that it would hurt?"

"Hurt?"

"To have you simply take off like that."

George nodded. "You could have at least left a note."

"I did. You didn't see it? I put it on the table in the kitchen, and then I said good-bye to Bruno...."

Realization struck them all at once, and all four of them turned to look at the dog. He'd left Colin's shoes and returned to his corncob and the fireplace, where he promptly fell asleep.

"I wonder if a certain overgrown mutt might have had something to do with its disappearance," George said.

Bruno sighed in his sleep and moved his corncob closer to him so that his chin was resting on it.

"So back to the notebook," Bud prompted.

"You know that my family owns a publishing company," Colin continued. "Not a big one, mind you, but when I read your notebook—"

"You read it!" Lolly sighed. "Well, why not. At this stage, it's probably public record, thanks to Bud."

"Hey!" Bud objected. "I said I was sorry."

"It doesn't undo what you did."

"You keep bringing it up, and I'll quit being sorry."

"That's what I mean. Living with you is a trial."

"Living with *you* is the crime."

"Stop!" George pounded the table with his hammy fist. "You two are the arguingest folks. Now stop so Colin can get on with what he has to say."

Lolly shot Bud one last *I'm not happy* glare, and he made a face at her.

Colin grinned and continued with his story. "I took your notebook back to New York and showed it to my cousin, and he suggested that we publish it as part of our Fairy Dreams line. Your notebook fits right into it."

"So what does that mean?" George asked, his face serious.

"It means we want Lolly to expand the book, and we'll publish it. To that end, I have a contract for you. We think it'll be a big hit."

She shook her head. "I'm not a writer."

He held up the notebook. "This says you are."

She looked at her brothers. "What do you think?"

"It's your decision," George said. "I think it's worth looking into."

"If someone is willing to pay you money for pink roses and lavender ponies or whatever this stuff is that you write, I say go for it." Bud grinned. "Actually, what I say is take the money and don't look back."

Money. She looked around the farmhouse, which had seemed so forlorn when they'd first arrived, before they filled it with voices and warmth and food.

"Is there money with this contract?" she asked. "I don't mean to be crude about it, but—"

"There is a modest amount as an advance. There should be royalties, too, once the book is published and sells enough to recoup the advance."

"Would it be enough that we could stay here?"

"As I said, it's modest, but you should be comfortable for the rest of the year. At least until next spring."

"Is it enough for all of us to stay here?"

He touched her hand, very lightly. "We should probably

talk about what you mean by 'all of us.'"

Her heart shivered. His gaze caught and held hers, and without looking away, she said, "Go outside, Bud and George."

"Why should I have to—" Bud began his litany of complaint, but George hustled him into his coat.

"Why don't you and I go take a look at that old barn and see how it's doing?" George asked his brother.

"Well, this is stupid. There's going to be snow all over it. We won't be able to see anything. Let's look at it tomorrow. I just got nice and warm, and I don't want to lea—"

George yanked his brother toward the door. "Again, for the twelve hundred millionth time, I apologize for my brother. You two take as long as you need and give us a holler when you're ready for us to come in."

When they'd left, Colin took her hand in his and dropped to the floor on one knee. Bruno woke up again and brought the chewed corncob to Colin.

"Ewww," Lolly said, kicking it out of the way. "They should have taken you, too, dumb dog."

"Lolly, put simply, I love you. I want to spend my entire life with you. Will you marry me?"

He reached into his pocket and pulled out a small box. Bruno stuck his snout right on it, but Colin adroitly pushed him away. "This isn't for you."

Lolly opened the box. Inside was nestled a ring, a layered combination of gold and silver with a diamond centered squarely on top of it. "Oh, Colin!"

"If you say yes, we can get married at any time. Tomorrow or next year or a decade from now. Whatever you say, my kind-hearted woman."

"I say yes," she said. "Yes to both contracts. Yes, yes, yes, yes, yes!"

She flung her arms around his shoulders, and he stood, holding her and kissing her. "Let them stay outside for a few more minutes," she said at last. "We have a lot of catching up to do."

epilogue

We are together at last, forever. Spring is the time of new beginnings, and we have chosen to unite our lives as life touches the earth again, as it does each year to remind us that God's love never leaves us, never forgets us, never overlooks us. We are His. We belong to Him. He has given us this love, and we consecrate this union to Him.

From the *Mankato Free Press*:

Eleanor Ann Prescott and Colin Edward Hammett, both currently of Valley Junction, Minnesota, were joined in Holy Matrimony on April 2, 1936, in the Community Church, Reverend William Wellman presiding.

Miss Prescott was presented for marriage by her brothers, George and Barnaby. Ruth Gregory was her attendant.

A dinner was served after the ceremony at the home of the bride.

Mr. and Mrs. Hammett will be at home on the Prescott family farm following a honeymoon trip to New York City.

The honeymoon in New York City had been wonderful. Lolly had met Colin's family and the details of opening a Minneapolis branch of the company were in the works. Within a few months they'd be moving there, but now she was back at home in Valley Junction, as Mrs. Colin Prescott.

The old house was actually cozy once Colin and her brothers finished the work in it. It had taken them all winter to refurbish it, but now it was charming. It was small but as Colin said, as long as Bruno stayed in the main house, it was large enough.

The thought of starting her married life in the same tiny house where her parents had begun theirs was wonderful. She couldn't imagine a better place.

As a wedding gift, she'd embroidered the Bible verse that had started Colin on the journey that led him to their home. It had taken two months and was a bit uneven in places where she'd had to undo the stitching several times, but it was truly a labor of love. George framed it and hung it in the dining room.

Blessed is the man that trusteth in the LORD, and whose hope the LORD is. For he shall be as a tree planted by the waters, and that spreadeth out her roots by the river, and shall not see when heat cometh, but her leaf shall be green; and shall not be careful in the year of drought, neither shall cease from yielding fruit. JEREMIAH 17: 7–8

"We got you something, too," Bud said. "Bring it in, George."

"You could help," his brother said through clenched teeth.

"I could. But I'm not." Bud grinned cheerfully at Lolly.

George muttered as he muscled a small table from the corner. "We took the fence post with the cat carved on it and made it into the base of this table. See?"

Lolly sank to her knees and traced the outline of the cat. "Kind-hearted woman. I love it! Thanks so much, you two!"

"It was my idea," Bud said.

"I did the work," George countered. "You couldn't be bothered to—"

"Oh, you did not do the work. I did it. You were busy making googly eyes at Ruth and sucking down colas and planning your own wedding while I was at the hardware store getting the sanding—"

"Stop!" Colin held up his hand, laughing. "We get the idea. It's from both of you."

Lolly interrupted. "Wait. Did I hear the word *wedding*?"

"You did. We're planning for October, when the harvest will be over. You and Colin will be in Minneapolis by then, so we can live in our house. Bud can stay with us, too."

Lolly threw her arms around her older brother. "I'm so glad!"

"If I tell you that I'm taking Sarah Fallon to the church social next week, would I get a hug, too?" Bud asked.

"Of course!" She followed through on her promise and nearly choked when Bud squeezed her so hard he lifted her right off the floor.

"We have something else, too," George said, handing Lolly a large flat packet.

She opened it. "Look, Colin!" It was their marriage license, framed and under glass.

"It's got the glass over it," Bud said, "so Bruno can't eat it."

The dog cocked his ear at the mention of his name.

"Let's put it here," she said as she put it over the fireplace. "Safe and sound, so nobody will knock into it. And where Bruno can't possibly reach it!"

The dog sighed and lay down to sleep, but if anyone had been watching, they'd have noticed that one eye didn't close all the way but was instead tracking a path from the table to the couch to the fireplace—all to check out the treat that was hanging over it.

A Letter To Our Readers

Dear Reader:

In order that we might better contribute to your reading enjoyment, we would appreciate your taking a few minutes to respond to the following questions. We welcome your comments and read each form and letter we receive. When completed, please return to the following:

Fiction Editor
Heartsong Presents
PO Box 719
Uhrichsville, Ohio 44683

1. Did you enjoy reading *Kind-Hearted Woman* by Janet Spaeth?
   ❏ Very much! I would like to see more books by this author!
   ❏ Moderately. I would have enjoyed it more if

   _____

   _____

   _____

2. Are you a member of **Heartsong Presents**? ❏ Yes ❏ No
   If no, where did you purchase this book? _____

   _____

3. How would you rate, on a scale from 1 (poor) to 5 (superior), the cover design? _____

4. On a scale from 1 (poor) to 10 (superior), please rate the following elements.

   ____ Heroine   ____ Plot
   ____ Hero   ____ Inspirational theme
   ____ Setting   ____ Secondary characters

5. These characters were special because? _____
_____
_____

6. How has this book inspired your life? _____
_____
_____

7. What settings would you like to see covered in future
Heartsong Presents books? _____
_____
_____

8. What are some inspirational themes you would like to see
treated in future books? _____
_____
_____

9. Would you be interested in reading other **Heartsong
Presents** titles? ❏ Yes ❏ No

10. Please check your age range:
❏ Under 18   ❏ 18-24
❏ 25-34   ❏ 35-45
❏ 46-55   ❏ Over 55

Name _____
Occupation _____
Address _____
City, State, Zip _____
E-mail _____

PRAIRIE HEARTS

Three women of the 1890s dream of romantic adventure, but can they possibly find it in the small town of Cedar Bend, Kansas? When Carrie Butler's runaway buggy is stopped by a handsome drifter, she believes her dreams have come true. But John Thornton has come to dig up old secrets in town. Mariah Casey has found purpose in mothering an orphan, but romance eludes her until she meets a handsome rancher. But when Mariah clashes with Sherman Butler's daughter, romance may escape her again. Joanna Brady's prayers for excitement seem to be answered in the appearance of a dangerous wrangler. But Clay Shepherd is not the marrying type.

Please send me _____ copies of *Prairie Hearts*. I am enclosing $7.97 for each.
(Please add $4.00 to cover postage and handling per order. OH add 7% tax.
If outside the U.S. please call 740-922-7280 for shipping charges.)

Name_____

Address _____

City, State, Zip _____

To place a credit card order, call 1-740-922-7280.
Send to: Heartsong Presents Readers' Service, PO Box 721, Uhrichsville, OH 44683

HEARTSONG
PRESENTS

If you love Christian romance…

$10.99

You'll love Heartsong Presents' inspiring and faith-filled romances by today's very best Christian authors…Wanda E. Brunstetter, Mary Connealy, Susan Page Davis, Cathy Marie Hake, and Joyce Livingston, to mention a few!

When you join Heartsong Presents, you'll enjoy four brand-new, mass-market, 176-page books—two contemporary and two historical—that will build you up in your faith when you discover God's role in every relationship you read about!

Imagine…four new romances every four weeks—with men and women like you who long to meet the one God has chosen as the love of their lives…all for the low price of $10.99 postpaid.

To join, simply visit www.heartsong presents.com or complete the coupon below and mail it to the address provided.

✂ -

YES! Sign me up for Heartsong!